TARD

DEL STAECKER

RED ENGINE
PRESS
PRINTED IN THE USA

TARD

Del Staecker

COVER DESIGN BY SANDRA MILLER

EBOOK ISBN: 978-1-943267-95-8

PAPERBACK ISBN: 978-1-943267-93-4

LIBRARY OF CONGRESS CONTROL NUMBER: 2022930287

TEXT COPYRIGHT © 2022 BY DEL STAECKER

FIRST EDITION ~ JANUARY 2022

10 9 8 7 6 5 4 3 2 1

PUBLISHED BY RED ENGINE PRESS
PITTSBURGH, PENNSYLVANIA USA

PRINTED IN THE USA ~ ALL RIGHTS RESERVED.

WHAT OTHERS ARE SAYING

"A masterly and thought-provoking tale of redemption and the spiritual truth that is there for the taking, hiding in plain sight, if we open our minds."

> ~ *Howard Owen, recipient of the Dashiell Hammett*
> *Prize and author of the widely acclaimed*
> Willie Black *series.*

* * *

"*TARD* is an unconventional story, a dreamlike meditation on traversing love, cruelty, and self-awareness, asking us to engage in the difficult adventure of self-exploration to discover our true spiritual nature and live the only life we have been given."

> ~ *J. Madison Davis, Edgar nominated author of*
> The Van Gogh Conspiracy

* * *

"A work of great imagination, from the farmlands of Lancaster County, PA, to the cornfields of Iowa, *TARD* is a grand, devastating story of sin and forgiveness and of the redemptive power of storytelling; it is about what blinds us from the miracles in our midst and what opens our eyes to realizing heaven on earth."

> ~ *Jim Zervanos, Author of the novel* LOVE Park.

* * *

"This book is beautiful. I cried so much—ugly cry, beautiful cry, inspired cry."

> ~ *Sandra Miller Linhart, Award-winning Author of*
> Daddy's Boots *and* Frozen Tears

TABLE OF CONTENTS

PROLOGUE

"From the moment you read these words I am in your mind." ~ Richard, a self-described former retard

FROM THE ARCHIVES OF THE *Lancaster Daily Journal*:

SPECTACULAR PHENOMENON APPEARS ABOVE CITY—A RARE ATMOSPHERIC PHENOMENON KNOWN AS A CIRCUMZENITHAL ARC, OR CZA, WAS OBSERVED YESTERDAY AT 2:11 P.M. IN THE SKIES ABOVE LANCASTER, PENNSYLVANIA. THE INVERTED RAINBOW, OR GOD'S SMILE AS IT IS KNOWN IN LEGENDS AND FOLKTALES, IS AN EXTREMELY RARE OPTICAL EVENT. FEW PEOPLE HAVE OBSERVED ONE OF THESE SPECTAC-ULAR PROCEEDINGS DUE TO THE REQUIREMENT FOR

A UNIQUE COMBINATION OF CIRCUMSTANCES FOR ONE TO FORM.

A CIRCUMZENITHAL ARC IS UNLIKE A COMMON RAINBOW, WHICH APPEARS OPPOSITE THE SUN. INSTEAD, THE CZA IS CENTERED AROUND THE SKY'S ZENITH, FORMING ONLY UNDER THE RIGHT CONDITIONS AND WHEN THE SOLAR ANGLE IS LESS THAN THIRTY-TWO DEGREES. A VIBRANT COLORED ARC APPEARS WHEN MILLIONS OF SMALL SIX-SIDED ICE CRYSTALS THE SIZE OF GRAINS OF SALT ARE FOUND AT 20-25,000 FEET ALTITUDE IN CLEAR SKIES. SUNLIGHT IS BENT AFTER ENTERING THE CRYSTAL'S BROAD SIDES AND REFLECTED OUT THEIR EDGES. MAGNIFICENTLY SEPARATED COLORS, PURER THAN THOSE IN THE TYPICAL APPEARANCE, CREATE A REVERSE RAINBOW WITH THE COLOR RED APPEARING CLOSEST TO THE EARTH.

VETERAN WGAL CHANNEL 8 TV METEOROLOGIST AND SKY WATCHER WARREN MICHAELS DESCRIBED HIS EXPERIENCE ENTHUSIASTICALLY, "THE ODDS OF THIS TYPE OF OCCURRENCE HAPPENING ARE NEARLY IMPOSSIBLE TO CALCULATE AND SOME OBSERVERS HAVE CALLED IT A MIRACLE. INDEED, IT WAS AN AMAZING SIGHT TO WITNESS, AND IN SOME INEXPLICABLE WAY I FEEL BLESSED TO HAVE DONE SO."

I Am Richard, Smarter Than Before

"A weed is a flower yet to be recognized for its value."

PLATO TOLD US THE BEGINNING is the most important part. So, that is where I'll start.

But how does one describe the indescribable? Explain the unexplainable?

The pat answer is to do the undoable.

Yeah—sure thing—easy said is not easily done.

Some memories should be totally forgotten. Some are meant for you to see once and then move on. The best ones are magnets that pull you in time and again, allowing you by repetition to become a good storyteller, sharing what happened—just the way it came down. Simply serve it up raw. Ungarnished. Tell the truth—pure and simple. However, the truth, pure and simple, is a rare commodity. And it is difficult to unbiasedly explain a situation while being on the inside because there is that not-so-small matter of overcoming subjectivity, as in this situation. Truth becomes complicated when the storyteller is part of the tale.

Honesty aside, it is not an easy matter to expose oneself. Traveling with truth can be a lonely road, especially in an insane world. Double that when people label you CRAZY.

And, as difficult as it might be to explain the inexplicable, one has to try. The best I can do is to just get the story right—share the facts. Let you, the listener, sort out the truth. But just now, I need to get something out of the way.

"Do you believe in miracles?"

Now wait—don't roll your eyes. Perhaps I should have asked my question differently. My question should have been, "Do you believe wondrous things really happen?"

Let me explain.

Halting the procession of the sun across the sky, or parting the Red Sea, those are *big event* miracles. That's not the sort of thing I'm referring to. For the big event type of miracle, a large part of the believing is simply in the seeing. But I've never seen one.

What touched my world was something else—a wondrous personality influencing others and seeding goodness. In the instance at hand, instead of a big event miracle, I want to share something much more subtle that flows within multiple occurrences—a wondrous theme, a trend of total goodness. That's my idea of miraculous.

Where I am coming from is more than mere wordplay, technicality, or jargon. It's more than a one-time event. Smaller in size, yet more in depth and length of its effect. Something in time—recurring. Think more like *Essence*. Spirit. Perhaps the *Truth* on display, weaving its way through existence, walking and talking god-like amongst us. A real *sustained* miracle, not just a one-off.

I would not be the least bit upset should you press me with, "Do you *really believe* in that sort of nonsense?"

My answer is, "Yes!" Because I believe in special people influencing the fabric and flow of time. They make wondrous things occur.

In fact, I know one such person quite well—my friend Matt.

This is his story.

* * *

PEOPLE ALWAYS SAID I WAS retarded. Nowadays "mentally disabled" is the polite and more acceptable term. But whatever words people use to describe you, the treatment is the same.

Now I am smart enough not to be called retarded or mentally disabled at all. Fact is, I am no longer retarded. Actually, I am pretty smart. Granted, I do have gaps. For instance, based on my lack of inter-action, I don't understand the whole male-female thing. I'm certain you'll notice more of my short-comings as we go along, but I'm getting better. I'm developing—making advances. An explanation of my progress is what I want to share. Matt's the cause.

Back to my wondrous-thematic-experience versus a one-off event.

I call my entry into the wondrous flow created by Matt, *The Incident*. It marks the beginning of my not being mentally disabled. Obviously, it's important to me, but it is just the beginning part of the wondrous story I'll unwind for you. Today, as *Now Me*, I'm smart enough to tell you the details, to serve the truth up raw, explain the unexplainable, and recount what happened to me and my best friend Matthias Emanuel Mueller.

My part in the story starts the day that Kyle Rattigan brained me with a rock. The one propelled by his rage at being bested by a freakish little man-child—my friend Matt. And although that blow was painful and near deadly, it really was a blessing—one that changed many lives—part of the flow. Some lives changed for the best that day. Some changed not so good.

I'll give the entire account soon but, in a nutshell, Rattigan's uncontrolled rage left me unconscious with blood seeping from my severely damaged head. Dazed. Bleeding. Racked with pain. Zonked, as they say. I was as close to *lights out* as a finger on a switch. Slipping away, perhaps headed for a dirt nap, I heard a voice.

Betcha it's no surprise to you the voice I heard was—Matt's.

"Richard, I'm here for you. You'll be fine—just do as I say."

That voice, strong and clear, passed through my pain like a breeze through a brand-new screen door. It penetrated my brain and turned a couple of my long-disused circuits to the ON position.

There I was, seriously injured, out on the narrow-est of ledges, clinging to life. And after spending my existence up to that time being identified as retarded, I heard Matt say, "Think!"

No one had ever spoken to me with such intensity, clarity, compassion—no—it was Love. Matt spoke

Love. We're not talking bromance. It was a god-like presence communicating directly with me. I knew I mattered. Clear as a bell, I knew he loved me.

Matt went on, "Richard, think as hard as you can. Think about something wonderful—somewhere you have always wanted to be—a magic spot."

Just imagine the situation. I'm headed toward death's door and Matt wants me to use *my mind* to expand the borders of my universe. Me? Hey, Matt—remember? I'm retarded.

Granted, at that time my existence did need a lot of expansion. I did as I was told. I thought of a magic spot—a place occupied by Indians, pirates, and Lost Boys. It was *my* happy place.

As if he could read my mind, Matt knew I was ready. He commanded, "Go there! Now!"

I did.

And, as you shall come to know, his intervention created a chain-reaction of wonders beyond belief. Because of him, that rock traveled through the air without effect. Yet, it changed everything. Paradox? That rock changed nothing but my life.

I understand if you have trouble understanding or appreciating what Matt accomplished. It's exactly the sort of situation he initiates all the time. Matt is like that—always the positive catalyst—an incremental embodiment of a miracle. A game-changer for Good.

Back to my refuge seeking. To be clear, I did not escape to an animated cartoonish Neverland. Following Matt's order, I went to live with the *actual* Peter and the *real* Lost Boys.

Here is the how and why: In the excuse called a classroom, where I was warehoused each day with the other short-bus riders, we had many times over seen the original 1950's version of *Peter Pan*. We saw real people, not cartoon characters, playing the parts.

The exposure was not performed as an act of kindness. It was simply "toss in a tape" daycare. You know—better living through television babysitting. It's popularly practiced at institutions and homes alike.

The result of so many viewings was that I became an idiot-savant-Neverland-expert with a penchant for fairy dust and flight. So, naturally my "challenged intellect" thought it was real. And on the occasion of *The Incident*, Matt helped me make it so. Mind over matter—in action. You ought to try it.

Back to *The Incident*.

At the time I was as near brain-dead as anyone could be. My body hung on, but I was elsewhere. An ambulance arrived. On-site care. ER. Hospital. Coma. Done. It's no big surprise in the end I was placed on a pallet at the Parker Rehabilitation Home to wither and die. I'd say it met the definition of "Life Sucks."

Everyone except Matt gave up on me. He disappeared from our hometown for a while due to the commotion set in place by *The Incident*—it's part of this long story. But he returned and has been with me almost every day since I went "lights out" to the rest of the world. I could always hear him. Still can. Still do.

My injury was a match. His directive was the fuel for my miraculous change. At first, even with a limited capacity for thought, I was just like many people shocked to find his brand of positive thinking works. But in time, it sunk into me. If you lay horizontal an inordinate length of time, with nothing but a ceiling above you with endless bed sores, boredom gets your mind working in some pretty amazing ways. Mentally, I caught up. Yep—amazing!

How amazing? Enough that I learned to fly.

It's true.

I *can* fly. I really can.

And while you're trying to absorb that, let me tell you in addition to flying—I travel through time and space. I bet you think I'm crazy. I understand. But crazy is just another form of being…the crazy kind.

I believe if something can be explained or experienced, even if it sounds weird, it's not crazy. If you're thinking, *This guy is full of crap,* I don't blame you. If I did not experience flying firsthand, I'd think the same. I would be more than skeptical. In fact, I'd be super skeptical. Especially if I was aware of the physical and mental circumstances of the person making such a claim. My response is that you have to recognize your own boundaries and understand even the craziest ideas do exist outside of boundaries, borders, and limits. In the act of believing, we can escape the confines of the material world and use our consciousness to tap into—regain—many forgotten abilities, such as traveling through time and space.

How can I fly while comatose and totally paralyzed, plus being diagnosed as retarded? My best explanation is that by doing what Matt told me, I move from one reality tunnel to another.

Too simple?

Just so. It *is* simple. With my mind, I think and then it happens. It just is. It is a fact. A *simple* fact. I travel through time and space just by using my mind.

I know you are about to roll your eyes again, but don't. Let me tell you what I know. Polite society benignly does away with rejects like me. It's true. Just as soon as they decide to nudge us toward expiring, after "doing the right thing," all their angst is politely spent. It would be ever-so-convenient for them if people like me did not exist.

My family felt that way and quickly signed me over to the system. Lack of money, shame, just being uncomfortable—they had enough. They would not admit it openly, but they hoped I would just go away—die.

But I did not die.

Although my injury was severe, my body was strong. There was a spark of life in me. Matt fanned that spark and I learned to fly and move about through time using my mind. He has taught me that if you do not know such things, you cannot choose, and without a choice—to believe that you can fly and do many wondrous things—you won't. You can't. No choice equals no choosing.

Matt gave me choice.

What's my secret? How I did I get to Neverland? Astral projection? That's what some would call it. But I believe it is more than that—it's not just an event miracle. More like a mysterious process, akin to the wondrous thing it is within—Matt.

He is my reason for sharing all this with you.

It could be fledgling soul travel. I'm too busy doing it and just know I spurt and sprint about the spiritual realm in search of something. Neverland was my first stop. I suspect there will be a final destination at some point.

Once in Neverland, I found I was so unlike the Lost Boys (who fell out of strollers and were unclaimed by their parents—people who failed

CHILDREARING 101). I got there on my own—with the help of a rock and a good friend. I suppose appearing in Neverland on my own steam impressed Peter and led him to allow me to fly next to him on many adventures. The Lost Boys never did fly with us—ever. Maybe Peter did not trust them to fly because they were careless enough to get lost.

What adventures! If it weren't for Matt, I'd just be a slab of meat kept alive in an underfunded second-rate institution, merely a result of greed within the medical care establishment's reimbursement system. Instead, I traveled to Neverland, lived with Peter and the Lost Boys, and most importantly, I chose not to be retarded any more. But my tale is really of little matter. Matt's story is more important.

I could explain more, but right now I am getting the urge to move about. You know, fly out of there, here and now—do my flying thing. Mostly I go to where the people and things I care about are located. Sometimes it's in the present, sometimes not. I am at times the observer and at others a participant. But always, I see the things that are important and all of them are linked to Matt.

There are a gazillion things I want to share about Matt—how he was born under a special sign from nature, how he is so smart, and why he sees and thinks so differently than everyone else. Take time for example. When Matt says it's time to leave, he has three meanings. When he says, "I'm going," he means to leave in a couple of minutes, maybe as long as five or ten minutes. "I'm going, now," means Matt will leave in a minute or less, and when he says, "I'm going *now*, *now*," he means *right* now.

I don't want to babble on, but you need to know how excited I am. Did I tell you how surprised and happy I am you're here? Did you get here like me—through some wondrous process? Did a big event whoosh you here? Or are you dreaming? It makes no difference really—because I'm busting out all over to show you *my ability* to move about.

Come on—I'll talk along the way.

Let's go *now, now*—to where and when I got hurt.

* * *

DETAILS OF THAT SPECIAL DAY

I'VE LEARNED A LOT SINCE the days people called me retarded. I can't blame them. They were not wrong, then. Now is different—in my mind I am beyond all that. I hold no grudges. I have grown. As I said, I have gaps, but I am learning.

My coming back to the day it all started brings to mind many of the ideas I've learned since then. Important ones—like this: Children absorb the sights, sounds, smells, and emotions around them. They take in everything. They mimic. Then they learn by doing themselves what they mimicked.

Children must be civilized, melded into society. They must be socialized, blended into the tribe. Sadly, their mentoring is often placed in the hands of immature kids a few inches further along the learning curve.

Lacking judgment, the older children's reasoning skills are not fully developed. Yet they lead the way. Latchkey kids learning from their own. Children teaching children.

It's a recipe for disaster.

* * *

AFTER DISMISSAL FROM THEIR COSTLY private school, a well-dressed small herd of demon-children sauntered down President Avenue, carrying on as if the neighborhood was their private property. In their defense, their attitudes were merely a reflection of their parents' opinions. In the eyes of the neighborhood, the children were merely "spirited, good kids". Indeed, they could "do nothing wrong". They were deemed "admirable".

They were anything but, and on that day, they aimed to prove it.

In any other neighborhood they'd be labeled a street gang, or worse—a pernicious horde of hellions on the prowl, crawling like vipers through comfortable streets. This batch of faux-children only appeared to be young humans. In reality, they were small venomous demons trick-or-treating their way through a world of privilege. For them, every day was Halloween. They only donned thin veneers of civility as costumes, while feasting on the bread of indifference and shame.

The group, well-groomed and pampered from afar by absentee parents, knew nothing about life's pains and wants. And although they dreamt and possessed an untold number of selfish desires, their longings were nothing more than tantrums demanding instant gratification. Truly, demons posing as children—the toxic spawn of their environment, nothing more. And perhaps, a great deal less.

Although young, they were already perfect actors. They knew how to give their parents and the world at large the desired performance.

Their teachers were also great fans because they, too, secretly wanted what the parents had—More. And they naturally and dutifully sought the approval of their "economic betters".

The only ones not fooled by their acting was the children themselves. The fooling had not yet begun within the group. An embryonic and unsophisticated Paganism was their operative creed. They loved nothing but themselves and did not know what they wanted.

Unsatisfied, they were simply vicious.

* * *

EACH DAY THE GROUP'S MOST malignant members loitered a half block south of Buchanan Street in an alley off President Avenue. Concealed by manicured hedges, the older boys consumed cigarettes and alcohol they had filched from unsuspecting parents. It was there the gang devised their attack plans. Anyone they disliked were targets. The more unsuspecting the better.

To fight boredom, and for sport, they bullied weaker males and molested innocent females. A pack of hyenas, the miniature sociopaths stalked and assaulted under a pecking order. The younger boys, fascinated by the dark profane side of life, learned through mimicry, and impatiently waited for their turn at the girls while standing guard at the alley's entrance.

On the day of The Incident, Kyle Rattigan, the gang's leader, barked orders upon sighting a familiar yellow vehicle.

"Get ready! Do it as I planned."

Soon, their prey—the disabled children of the neighborhood—would be delivered by the much-mocked *short bus*. Then the fun would start.

"They're nothing but fuckin' rejects." Rattigan loved to use language unsanctioned in his home and school. "Never should've been born—fuckin' cripples

and retards. Shouldn't be allowed to breathe our air."
He found that bending the rules and using language
in doing so gave him power over the gang. "You're
so much better than *Them*." he yelled.

The gang roared approval. When false information makes *you* look good, you're likely to believe it.

Rattigan pointed at the braking bus as it
approached the curb. "Don't let the Big Fucker get
away."

His aspiring second-in-command, Jude Blackman,
dutifully answered with enthusiasm, "We know what
to do." Adding, "We'll smile, so the bus driver thinks
we're helping them get home."

"Fuckin' rejects. They ain't human." Rattigan
shot a thumbs-up sign to gin-up the little demons.

Primed. Inspired. Their hungry eyes watched for
their meal to arrive. Rattigan's power over them came
in the delivery of thrills. He was an inch ahead of
them on the depravity curve. Lies barked as orders
were at the heart of his power. Rattigan knew those
who get you to readily believe lies can get you to
commit atrocities, for people are tremendously intol-
erant in their hearts and less able to accept those
who differ.

As the small yellow bus stopped, the gang waved
a feinted welcome.

"Remember they ain't human," Rattigan repeated. "They ain't like us."

The vehicle's door opened, allowing four passengers to disembark. Matthias, a boy of perhaps twelve or thirteen, wearing a backpack and possessing the distinct physical characteristics of Down Syndrome, stepped to the street. Two girls immediately followed.

The first, Karen Parks, was similar in appearance to the boy, but older, almost an adult. The second girl, Mya Krim, bright-eyed and alert, was stooped over by a pronounced physical deformity. Her tortured body, wrapped by a torso brace, strained not to imitate the shape of a comma. Only physically disabled, she quickly surmised the hovering gang was a threat. She moved to escape the scene as rapidly as her misshaped body would allow.

Her path was unfortunately blocked.

"Not so fast," Rattigan ordered. "We can't have you gimping home to tattletale about our little get-together." He shoved her toward two underlings and coolly said, "Get her out of sight in the bushes. Make it hard for her to see anything."

The boys did as they were told but were not happy.

"Not worth fooling with," one told another.

"Yeah," was uttered in sad agreement.

The disappointed minions moved into the alley and shoved Mya into the hedgerow, facing her away from what was about to happen.

"At least we got a view from here," one said.

"Yeah—big deal," was the other's answer. "We get to nursemaid a gimp and they get all the fun."

The final person to exit the bus was Richard Bettis. The *Then Me*.

My family called me Richie. I prefer Richard. Makes no difference—they had pretty-much given up on me even then. I'm tall. Wide-shouldered. Thick, not fat. For my entire school life, I rode the short bus. Shunned. Mocked.

After graduation I was headed to a group home, to begin lifelong semi-incarceration as a cast-off. To be culled from the human herd. My future was not bright.

Although I was a retarded man-child, back then my IQ was high enough to lead me to the obvious conclusion I was the target.

Rattigan stepped forward, grabbed my arm, and led me into the alley.

* * *

FROM ME NOW

C OULD YOU HOLD ON A moment? Nausea is physical. Embarrassment is a powerful emotion. When the two combine I get confused. Seeing myself as I was makes me queasy. The first time I came back to visit this day, I blacked out—I mean totally out. You being here has me off my game. I need to detach some, so it doesn't hurt so much.

I don't believe I can go on watching.

Give me a minute.

At times, this flying-thing is more than weird. I see things happening as if I am me. But other times

I'm not me—I'm another person just watching. In literature it's called *point of view*. Matt taught me that.

Maybe it's because you are here with me that I experience the difference more strongly. Sometimes I see and sometimes I am. Confusing, but it's how I see and live here and there at the same time. Then Me—Me Now—Then Me—Me Now.

*   *   *

BACK IN THE ALLEY

RATTIGAN OOZED VENOMOUS CHARM, "HELLO, Richie." He smiled. "We've been waiting for you."

His smile grew. A spider watching its web. A snake hypnotizing prey.

"Ah—Ah—Ah—" Richard (Then Me) moaned. He knew the gang. He had painfully experienced their attentions several times.

The gang joined with Rattigan and pushed Then Me and the others further down the alley. Matt and Karen were shoved along behind Then Me and the remainder of the gang fell in line. There was no escape.

Ten yards up the alleyway, out of sight from all eyes, the group stopped.

Matt proved uncooperative. He bravely struggled, but his guards were stronger.

Once all were in place, the gang looked to their leader for further instructions.

Rattigan shouted, "Pull down the big freak's pants."

His order caused several of the female gang members to loudly giggle.

One of them blurted, "Let's see it—*let's see his thing!*"

Richard stood frozen in place.

Rattigan pointed to one boy and calmly instructed, "Get out the camera. We're gonna take pictures of his dick."

Richard remained a statue. Dark electric energy filled the air. Girlish giggles ringed again, then they escalated.

The gang loudly cheered. "Rat-ti-gan! Rat-ti-gan! Rat—ti—gan!"

Bolstered by their chant, Rattigan egged them on. He bellowed, "Look! It's as big as a salami. Get a picture—get pictures of the whole damn thing. And his balls, too."

The dark energy intensified as laughter filled the alley.

Rattigan pointed at Karen. "Get ready, Girlie—your retarded pussy is next."

Terrified, Karen trembled. Tears ran down her cheeks. She pled, "Please, no, please. No! Please, please!" Her voice trailed off to where fear resides, and then multiples.

Addressing the quaking girl, Rattigan commanded, "Shut up—you fucking retard-bitch." He viciously slapped her with one hand, then with both. "Shut up! Shut up! Shut up!"

Karen whimpered. She did not beg. She could not scream. She whimpered more. The tempo and fury of Rattigan's slaps increased to match the chant of the gang.

"Rat-ti-gan! Rat-ti-gan!! RAT-TI-GAN!!!"

The mindless noise-chants reverberated through the alley until a voice, seemingly from the sky above, addressed Rattigan. The voice simply commanded, "STOP!"

It came from Matt who had slipped away from his distracted chanting guards. He repeated the order. "STOP! Stop hitting her."

After addressing Rattigan, Matt's next action was to place himself as a shield between the girl and her tormentor. Rattigan halted his assault and redirected its fury. He grabbed Matt by his hair and jerked him about. Matt resisted.

"You're pretty feisty—for such a little retard." taunted Rattigan. He punched Matt hard in the face and was surprised no plea for mercy came forth.

Instead, Matt sternly responded with another warning, "You must stop!"

"Stop?" Rattigan asked in mock surprise. "Or what?" He shoved Matt into the grasp of his two toughest crew members and yelled, "Hold him!"

Rattigan pummeled Matt's stomach with his fists. He swung again and again. Matt silently absorbed the blows.

Out of breath, Rattigan gasped, "Take… that… you…you…" He wheezed and uttered only the end of a word, "…'tard!"

Punctuating his last blow with a grin he shouted, "That's it! 'tard! That's what I'll call you. From now on *you are Tard!*"

"Tard! Tard!! TARD!!!" chanted the gang. Their response reinforced Rattigan's strength and effort.

"You *are* Tard!" He swung again, and yelled, "Tard!" Again, he swung and yelled, "Tard!"

The gang chanted, "Tard! Tard!! TARD!!!" With each exclamation of the name, Rattigan punched his target hard.

Matt took each blow with silent strength. He finally slumped to his knees. Rattigan, taking it as a sign of capitulation, relented and barked more orders.

"Get his backpack. Take whatever looks good."

The gang eagerly rummaged through Matt's belongings.

"Well?" Rattigan impatiently demanded. "What'd you find?"

"Nothing," came the disappointed reply. "There's just books and a pad with some notes."

"Books? What's a retard doing with books?" Rattigan leaned in toward Matt and sneered, "Look, *Tard*—if they don't come up with something good, I'll have Dave here take a picture of you kissing that big salami. Do you understand, *Tard*?"

He vigorously slapped Matt again and again.

After the fifth slap, Jude Blackman yelled, "That's enough—he's done."

"Stay out of this." Rattigan spat back.

Jude made a move toward Matt.

Rattigan raged, "Don't go near him."

Rattigan was rabid. He motioned for two boys to stand Matt up. "He's gonna learn who's boss. I'll beat the piss out of him and take a picture of him sucking—"

Rattigan did not finish.

As the guards lifted Matt, he continued his upward motion further and faster than expected. Matt head-butted one guard and then stomped the other's instep. The guards were more than surprised and immediately abandoned their holds. Matt jammed his fist into Rattigan's face,stopping him in mid-phrase. The half-finished sentence was punctuated by the crunch of mashed nose cartilage.

Blood spurted. Rattigan howled with pain. No one moved.

A whirlwind had been unleashed. And there were consequences.

Rattigan whimpered, proving that everyone is a tough guy until they get whacked in the face.

Matt, the former captive, stood above the bleeding boy. "I am sorry. Really, I am. But I told you to stop and you chose not to."

The gang members did not move to assist Rattigan. Matt emanated strength and control. They were awed by his actions, paralyzed by the tone and seriousness of the words spoken by the dwarfish hero. An intended victim had vanquished their leader.

Rattigan, the one they had feared for so long, was relegated to the bottom of the heap.

Matt collected his companions.

Grabbing Richard's and Karen's hands, he calmly told them, "It's time to go." He called for Mya in the hedge, "Come! I will protect you."

She emerged from the hedge to be led away with the other wards.

* * *

THE GANG REMAINED SILENT. NOT one interfered with the departing captives. A barrier had been breached. Awe scented the air. No one had ever challenged Rattigan.

None of the gang assisted their fallen leader.

One clearly disappointed gang member sighed, "I guess the fun's over."

Another simply exclaimed, "Damn!"

A third remarked, "Tard really cleaned Rat's clock." He puffed up with pride in using the two nicknames.

Laughter erupted, then grew. The group circled the crumpled leader.

Rattigan cowered, fearing he was now the prey. Through bloodstained hands covering a mangled nose he whined, "Don't call me Rat. I told you never to call me that."

An emboldened gang member taunted, "You're such a pussy, *Rat!*"

Another snidely added, "*Rat* got whooped—by a retard."

Rattigan could not reply. His power was gone. Everyone knew it.

As if instructing a class, Matt declared with authority, "It's over," and turned away to shepherd his small flock toward the street.

* * *

POWER DOES NOT RESPECT A vacuum. Jude Blackman, the previous Number Two quickly claimed the vacancy atop the gang.

"Listen up! I'm the boss now."

No one objected. Jude's chest swelled.

Searching eyes fell on the new chief. The transfer of leadership was complete. It was a modern version of an age-old rite. The King is dead—long live the King.

Jude immediately applied the authority of his position. "Stop!" he shouted to the departing short-bus passengers.

Matt looked back.

Jude grabbed the puzzling contents of the rifled backpack, and asked, "Are these books *yours*?"

"Yes," Matt walked back to retrieve his property.

Examining the books, Jude countered with skepticism, "*Really*, Tard?"

"Yes. I said so." Matt took the books and his notepad. He placed the items into his backpack and swung in onto his shoulder.

"They're encyclopedias." Jude exclaimed with bewilderment.

"Yes."

A statement of fact. A revelation. Spoken with authority.

"But they hardly have any pictures." Jude pointed out. Then, mocking, "What do you use them for—paper weights?"

Matt calmly answered, "I read them."

He turned and walked away to rejoin and lead a still trembling Karen, a confused Richard, and a thankful Mya.

"Sure, *Tard*," Jude mocked, "and I'm the Tooth Fairy, right?"

Matt stopped again and walked back to face a very startled Jude. In defense of his new position Jude stood his ground.

Matt stared.

With a calm and stern voice, Matt said. "No. You are not the Tooth Fairy." He pointed at the bloodied ex-leader, his stare still focused on Jude. "Now, *you* are the leader. And as the leader, *you* should do no harm to others—it's the best rule to live by."

Challenged by the serious intelligence he faced, Jude stared at the incongruous being before him.

Matt stared back.

"You, a 'tard, think I can be a better leader—Huh?"

Silence. Deafening silence.

Finally, Matt replied, "Only you can answer that question."

Silence, again. Tension. Growing frustration.

Jude burst forth, "Get out of here, *Tard*." Pointing at the encircling gang members itching for action, "I'm serious, freak. Take that bigger freak and the cripples out of here before something really bad happens."

Matt stood his ground.

Jude threatened, "Go! Before I turn them loose on you, *Tard*."

"No," Matt replied, "You won't." He pointed again at the stunned and bleeding Rattigan. "That's what he would do. You must be better—much better." Matt spoke to Rattigan, "I *am* sorry I harmed you." Finally, to all, he declared, "My name is not Tard."

Matt led his frightened charges away.

As the gang assembled around its new leader, hoping to incite *something*, a frenzied chant filled the air. "Tard! Tard! Retard! You're nothing but a *reee—tard*."

Matt continued walking, not looking back.

When the gang realized their taunts were not effective, they turned their energy on Rattigan.

"Pussy! You're just a pussy." they screamed. "That retard showed you—you *pussy!*"

Rattigan squirmed.

Spurred on by his cowering, the gang intensified their taunts.

"Rat! Rat! Rat! Rat's a pussy. Nuthin' but a pussy."

Beleaguered. Broken. Rattigan begged, "Quit it—STOP! I'm not a pussy—I 'm NOT!"

"Yes, you are," Jude declared. "That retard got the better of you. He bested you."

The new leader had spoken. His followers readily believed. Rattigan continued to cower.

The gang reveled in their former leader's weakness and responded ever louder, chanting, "*Pussy—Pussy—Pussy*! Rat is nuthin' but a Pussy!"

Rattigan pled from weakness, "Stop. Stop. Just stop! I'm not a pussy. I'm not!" The pleading had no effect.

One of the gang members taunted Rattigan by tossing a rock at his feet. "If you're not a pussy—prove it."

The challenge was clear. The taunts were repeated from many mouths. "Prove you're no pussy—or you're a worthless piece of shit."

"Prove it! Prove it! Prove it!"

Ridicule can be a powerful weapon. At times there is no counter to its power; when seasoned with challenge, ridicule can produce violent, even deadly results.

Ridicule ruled the situation.

Rattigan's blood-smeared hand grabbed the rock. Filled with frenzy, he hurled it at Matt. The result was not as expected. In the venue of emotion over reason nothing is for certain. The Law of Unintended Consequences prevailed.

Propelled by hate for Matt, and shame-filled envy of Jude's new status, Rattigan's projectile went off course. Physics be dammed. Errant energy in action. A wild rock. A misguided missile. The projectile missed Matt and sailed on to find another target.

Karen screamed.

Mya covered her eyes.

Richard's head exploded.

Everyone watched blood spurt.

And, the giant man-child dropped to the ground like a puppet with cut strings.

* * *

COVERING TRACKS 101

I'M MORE THAN QUEASY EVERY time I come back to that day. Now Me does not enjoy observing what happened to Then Me. I suppose seeing oneself brutally injured can be a necessary evil if jumping through time and space is the blessing. At the end of my story, you can be the judge.

The second I hit the ground, the gang disappeared. Smoke in a hurricane. False courage on the run. "I didn't do nuthin'" at its best.

Although terrified, Karen immediately moved toward my seemingly lifeless form. Joined by Myra, the two girls each grasped a hand. Matt rested my head in his lap. He applied pressure to my wound.

For people with a strong sense of justice, this is the point in the story where the hero steps in to make everything okay.

That was what Matt did. He focused on me. The rock served as an exclamation mark for one young life—mine—and question marks for all the others. From that day onward all our lives moved forward—forever joined—with me as the observer, as well as participant.

Karen's scream did not go unheard. A resident of the neighborhood, the proverbial little-old-lady-peering-from-behind-her-curtains, alarmed by the intensity of Karen's vocalized horror, got involved—as involved as an anonymous 911 call can be.

The last thing I remember of that day, as Then Me, was hearing Matt's instruction to find my happy place.

As I went there, he whispered, "I'm sorry, Richard. I'm so sorry. The rock was meant for me. I promise no one will hurt you again—I promise."

I believed him. As far as the world was concerned, I was as close to being dead as anyone can be. In any other instance, it was then my lights should have gone out—forever.

When I fly through time, I find and follow the lives of those who were in the alley. Why? I do not fully understand. That day the world tilted and we all slid to the same corner of the game board. There Matt displayed his special nature.

If the event in the alley was a sentence, then the mis-thrown rock was its punctuation mark—and it made Matt what? The hero? The savior? Matt is the hub. The rest of us are merely spokes.

What happened after The Incident? Through my flying-thing, I'll show you what took place.

Word quickly traveled through the "better portion" of the community and the gang members' families were alerted, by friendly officials, that the after-school meeting spot was no longer a safe haven for their "spirited" children to do what they do—run amok and teach cruelty to one another. Importantly, without the slightest embarrassment for their hypocrisy, the same community-minded authorities immediately dispersed the passengers of the short bus into separate after-school treatment programs. Their families were persuaded it was "in everyone's best interest" to forget the event and move on. Hypocrisy with a kindness veneer.

Their question: What's to be done?

Answer: The usual. Nothing disguised in everything.

You can bet no grinding wheels of justice churned. Instead, the Powers That Be went to work, as is the custom. Status, wealth, influence—call it what you will—does what it does. Takes measures. Exerts influence. Protects progeny. Negates opposition. Shifts the focus. Assigns blame. Quashes stories. Molds the truth. Creates a narrative. Makes it yesterday's news. Forgets.

Remember, history is an agreed-upon lie.

The child-hyenas were lectured—ineffectively. Side glances, deaf ears, shoulder shrugs, and eye rolls are the practiced skills of mimics training to rule and ruin society. Moral Tone-Deafness taught in the "best" of homes for raising well-to-do sociopaths won the day. In sum, life for the privileged just went on. Repackaged.

The gang was not waiting for the short bus the following day. Nor would they do so again. But after time, actually quite soon, the gang reappeared. Under Jude Blackman's leadership, it relocated to nearby Buchanan Park where it assumed ownership of the pavilion, playground, and the adjacent lawns. The Park Punks, as they named themselves, avoided talking about the day Rat Rattigan got his nickname. Days fled, weeks became months, and all the gang's members put the incident in the past. They moved on.

Except Rattigan.

He festered.

More on this later.

Karen Parker could not forget the traumatic events of that day and often broke down, trembling as if that day was constantly present. For treatment, she was placed into a county-sponsored residence, where a monotonous crafts program attempted to fill her life with a flimsy goodness constructed of paste, blunt scissors, and crayons. Sporadically crying and trembling, Karen's fears prevented her from ever leaving the facility. One winter's day Karen gave up and suddenly died while assembling a chain made of colorful construction paper for the community's Christmas tree. She was sixteen.

Each day after school, Mya Krim was whisked to Lancaster General Hospital for participation in an experimental physical rehabilitation program. Her good fortune was made possible through the generosity of an anonymous benefactor. The effect of a regimen of grueling exercises was amazing. She no longer rode the short bus. A few years later, when Mya walked past the Park Punks, she was unrecognizable as their former prey. The green-eyed beauty known to her friends as Mick possessed a straight, firm, and desirable body.

As gang leader, Jude claimed many rights. One was to pursue Mick as his prize, but nothing came of it. Jude hopelessly grasped for her as she evaded him with a vengeance. Her heart was elsewhere. Their never-to-be relationship was visibly painful for Jude when Mick left for art school in Philadelphia. His disappointment at not winning her, and the anger he held for an overbearing father, was turned inward. It marked the beginning of his serious problem with alcohol.

Rattigan's new name stuck and he was relegated to hanger-on status with the gang and in life. Like a dimmed errant moon caught in Jude's gravitational field, Kyle "Rat" Rattigan spent his time orbiting his previous subordinate. He never shined again as a leader. He simply devolved. His constant fantasizing about regaining his former role and dreams of squashing the deformed bug he tagged Tard led him on a downward path. Failure. Juvenile delinquent. Petty criminal. More Failure. Jailed. Parolee. Journeyman Psychopath. His parents' resources disappeared in fruitless efforts to "reach" him. Eventually, Rat matriculated to prison.

The others? By the completion of their high school senior year, the gang's ranks were considerably thinned by drugs, car wrecks, STDs, and a list of rehab-boarding schools catering to delinquent rich kids moving too fast, doing too much, too soon.

With time, Matt's out-of-character display of intelligence and spunk became less and less a memory. That suited Matt's friends and protectors—among

* * *

YOU ALREADY KNOW WHAT HAPPENED to me. My traumatic head injury was a blessing in disguise. As I've shared, with Matt's prompting I was able to come out of my body for the first time that day. Matt encouraged and instructed me to do so. His will and spirit, simply enacted through his caring for me, bonded us in the continuance of the wondrous events that surround him.

At first, I was scared. My injury put me in a coma and as far as the world believes—except for you and Matt—I still am. In a miraculous way, he and I are kindred beings. I am a medical oddity. Matt is one, too. Maybe that's why he never gave up on me.

Matt stayed with me on that day. In the hospital he found a way to see me even though the staff pushed him away as being disabled and too young to be a 'real' visitor. However, he prevailed by persistence and intelligence. Matt is really smart.

At the Parker Home, where I've been all these years, he has continued to be my friend. Matt has access whenever he wants by playing a role. People see what they want to see. The staff assumes he is family and a harmless Down Syndrome man-child. So, they ignore him. It is easy—in Lancaster, almost everyone believes he is just an errand boy for vendors at the Central Market, where three days a week the oldest public market offers farm fresh produce and country-style baked goods.

Matt works for Elmer Stoltzfus, an Amish farmer. Matt hustles vegetables to restaurants and delivers cookies and pastries for Wendy's Homemade.

No one could imagine that under the disguise of a pen name, Matt is a financially successful author. All of this may seem strange. However, I have learned, especially in regard to Matt, strangeness is not in the nature of a thing, but in its relation to something else.

And there is nothing else in existence as strange as Matt.

* * *

A T THE PARKER HOME THEY don't care about me. I am unconscious and retarded—they have no idea what my mind is doing, or what I am capable of. In the world's opinion, I am a double loser, a cast-off. When Matt visits, he talks to me. I absorb everything he shares. He has visited me at least three times a week, every week for over a decade-and-a-half. Matt reads to me for hours on end. I don't think he ever sleeps. From a position of immense singular strength he thinks, reads, writes stories and novels, and acts upon the world around him. In my view—a one-man miracle.

Imagine all I have learned from Matt—important ideas from popular scholars. Like Carl Sagan, who said, "Somewhere, something incredible is waiting to be known." Or Albert Einstein, "When the answer is simple, God is answering." If it were not for Matt, I would be an ignorant disembodied fool merely taking up space. Or flying within it.

Take Quantum Physics. I understand the basic principles. They are within my grasp. Music theory, philosophy, history—loads of it—and much more fill my brain due to Matt. And it's not just high-level knowledge he has introduced me to.

There's trivia—interesting little-known facts and ideas—such as, people mistakenly believing it is impossible to hear the echo of a duck quack. But you can. In reality, the vibrations are so low it's too difficult for the common ear to pick up. Things like that.

And there's true silly stuff. Like—there are three kinds of toilet paper users—waders, wrappers, and folders. Waders use the most.

And more—such as, you are 18.37% more cool listening to *Deep Breakfast*. That's a semi-serious Matt Fact. Part truth, maybe, and part mirth.

Matt's humor is decidedly off-beat and quirky. Out of the blue he'll say something like, "The Origami store folded?" Or ask, "Did you know the Lone Ranger is in solitary confinement?" On arrival to my room, he might seriously exclaim, "Oh my God! Mr. Coffee just got mugged."

I wish he could see me laugh inside my coma. For me, I like when his jokes are bad-good. Like, "Jokes about German sausage are the wurst."

Fairy tales are fair game, too. I remember when Matt shared, "After trading the family cow for magic beans, Jack became paranoid. Repeatedly, Jack would say, 'I'm being followed by a bean stalker.'"

His favorite double-double entendre is, "Baby ducks can't engage in intercourse because their quacks are too small." He loves that one. And one time he shared the story about the world's greatest entrepreneur. His product? Instant water—you just add water.

Matt loves laughter. He believes it is the salve that soothes the scars of reality.

Then there is his love for baseball—it's almost beyond measure. I've grown to love it, too. I think his devotion to the sport came from the sandlot games he organized for us "retards" while waiting for the short bus at the end of our faux-school days. Our teacher/babysitters thought us incapable of such 'complex' behavior. Not so with Matt. He's a natural coach, and we learned easily under his loving instruction.

He taught me the nuances of the sport by explaining the game re-caps he read to me on those long nightly visits. In fact, my introduction to literature came by way of his favorite baseball books, such as, *Good Field No Hit*, *Shoeless Joe*, *The Boys of Summer*, and *The Great American Novel*. With Matt being so short, I think he got joy from there being a midget relief pitcher in that last one.

Intertwined and beyond books on baseball, we moved through offerings as varied as, *Zen and The Art of Motorcycle Maintenance*, *The Brothers Karamazov*, *Red Harvest*, *The Razor's Edge*, *Don Quixote*, *The Tin Drum*, *Zorba The Greek*, and *Slaughterhouse-Five*.

Several times he read to me *The Mayor Of Casterbridge*. Through it, I learned concepts such as sin, repentance, and forgiveness—all the pains, sorrows, and joys of life—which were delivered in spades when Matt read The Bible to me. I understood very little of it, but it was through his reading C. S. Lewis's *Mere Christianity*, the supernatural battle of good versus evil became clear to me. While listening to him read *The Master* and *Margarita* I perceived how evil works, and much appreciated its depiction of Satan having his way on Earth while wreaking havoc in Moscow.

Matt often says, "You can't beat the Russians for understanding the dark side."

Matt also enjoys science-fiction, like the classic *Stranger In A Strange Land* and *Dune*. And, when sci-fi edged into time travel, as in *Somewhere In Time* or *Now Wait For Last Year*, he'd give me a mini-lecture on how modern writers, with Vonnegut and Dick leading the way, introduced all sorts of mind-bending ideas into literature. Matt says reading is present consciousness entering the future through the consciousness of the past.

"You see," he'd whisper-shout in my sleeping ear, "creativity, consciousness—it's all connected. It's *truth* bubbling forth. Imagine historiography is explainable by *A Canticle For Leibowitz* where the sci-fi genre demonstrates concepts through the study of history? A terrific example of fiction influencing non-fiction. Great cross-pollination. It's *truth* yearning to touch us."

Matt reads much, absorbs everything, and is constantly thinking. Through him I know about Sun Tzu's *The Art Of War*, Thucydides' *History Of The Peloponnesian War*, Plato's *The Republic*, Thoreau's *Walden, The Analects Of Confucius*, and the wisdom of the longshoreman-philosopher, Eric Hoffer.

The list could go on and on. The key is Matt connects the dots within such a wide array of topics. Matt claims understanding the nuances of baseball opened his mind to do the same with the multitude of subjects he studied.

Genius? Yes, he sure is.

At the time, I was overwhelmed and just thrilled to be along for the ride.

Later, I understood he was my mentor—a loving guide to awaken me. He knew there was something in me beyond what the world saw. In his unique, comical, endearing way he probed, prodded, cajoled, and brought me up from the depths from which I had been relegated.

At times, he'd say, "Hey, Cupcake. You in there? C'mon out."

"Cupcake?" my emerging mind asked, "Why does he call me that?"

Then one day in a quip, Matt revealed his meaning.

"You know, Richard, a muffin is just a cupcake without sugar. And in this world, knowledge of the truth is the sugar." He let that thought sink in, and followed with, "I know you're in there. It's time to wake up the muffin—add some sugar—you know, the truth. Become a cupcake."

Then a lesson began.

Many more followed. For example, constant thoughts about weighty topics, Matt explained his understanding space is not empty. He told me, "It can't be empty, it contains the entire Universe."

Then, another other shoe-dropping-statement was, "Our journey in this material space, what we call our life, is tied to understanding that at the core of our essence the map is simultaneously our destination." He liked to say, "The so-called Kingdom of God is here, right now. You just have to look for it."

Matt's far-reaching thoughts were birthed in books. He enjoyed sharing the wonder found in their page—getting inside an author's head to expand his own consciousness. I think Matt was a beacon of light among we Cimmerians. See how he propelled my thoughts? Betcha you'll need to research that reference.

I, a muffin-soon-to-be-a-cupcake, was the perfect audience for Matt's ruminations. On one occasion, in an homage to the oft-told tale of Jack Kerouac typing an entire book on a single spool of stationery, Matt read *On The Road* to me in one sitting. And, try as I might—and I did—I could never fly through time to catch up with Kerouac's odyssey. Similarly, I never could join Ken Kesey and the Merry Pranksters on their bus.

Some trips are meant for others to take, but it does not lessen the need to know and learn from their experiences.

Learning about and empathizing with others can ease difficult travel along your own path. Study. Contemplate. Empathize. Know. Grow. Grow some more. Grow a pair. Get mad. Love. Remember the soul has no ethnicity or race. *Another Country, A Day In The Life Of Ivan Denisovich*, and *Bury My Heart At Wounded Knee* revealed that for me. Sometimes, no matter how hard you try, you cannot walk in another's shoes. But you have to try. Fail. Try again. And again—and again. That's Matt talking—through me.

For his "go to" book, to soothe and comfort us both, he read *Shoeless Joe* to me so many times I lost count.

He told me, "Richard, this is not just about baseball, or a father and son reconciling. It's about the supernatural becoming and being real. When we have desire and hope—dreams *do* come true. And when dreams become reality, we bask in love and experience the joy of being at home with the primal force—our creator."

I fly because of this. You being here is part of that, too.

Another book Matt read quite often to me is, *I Heard The Owl Call My Name*—a story of family, home, and love. It has the most bittersweet of endings. It is also about faith and the end becoming the beginning which is also the end.

My transformation, developing and growing from Then Me to Me Now, was a process that took place with Matt in a chair reading under the light of a monstrous junkyard metal lamp he had installed in my room. It's what I see from above when I fly.

Best of all my experiences with Matt, I love when he reads to me something he wrote himself. Imagine, a well-known author—one whose true identity is hidden—reading to a comatose test audience—me!

His insight into the human experience is truly amazing. Here is the first story he shared with me. It's short, but I really like it because it is about a writer, and that's what Matt is at heart.

* * *

My Counselor, My Characters, and Me

by Otto Janus (Matt's pen name)

I N TRUTH, SEEING A MENTAL health professional, a shrink, is just paying someone to be your friend.

Here's the way I see it: When your regular friends and family reach the tolerance limit for your writer-based weirdness, a paid counselor is the back-up. For a fee, your shrink friend will listen to any and all topics that leak from your mind and freak out the normal folks living around you.

It is a fact, people love to tell anyone they know, even strangers, that you, the writer, are their close, personal friend. They enjoy sharing details of the neat parts of you being a writer—the awards, appearances and signings, and most of all, the royalty checks. Your success is their success. Sign a new deal and see how popular you become. People love to pal around with an artist who actually gets paid to be one.

Friends love to know and share the safe and interesting parts of you. But they do not want the weird or dark stuff. You take that material to the ear it cannot be turned off. And you clearly know it is time to see a mental health provider when your regular friends say, "You need help" and mean it. My time came more than a year ago when I was wrapped up in my characters to the point those around me thought I was losing it for real. When no one would meet me for a beer, I caved and paid a counselor to be my friend.

My books are known and appreciated for their compelling characters. When I make a presentation, or do a signing, readers always ask me about the people of my books rather than the plots. I'm fine with that. For me plot is just the stuff interesting people do.

My counselor loves to hear about my characters. At first, he believed, or wanted to believe, all were based upon people I made up. He had the idea my imagination, not reality, was their source of being. He has learned otherwise.

During a session I mentioned two of my characters woke me up one night to discuss what I had in mind for them. They were not pleased with the way things were going in the plot and had some suggestions of their own. I jumped into the conversation to make it a three-way exchange. I told them I am not God, but God is me—at least in their world. They didn't buy that. Free Will at work. In the end, the plot was eventually tweaked to their satisfaction. Such is life.

Hearing this, my counselor took a lot of notes. He asked a lot of questions, too.

"Do you think your characters are real?" he asked.

"Sure—why not?" The note-taking cranked up to a higher level. "But they are not really my characters," I informed him.

"What do you mean?" my counselor asked.

"I'm their storyteller. I just record what they do."

His note pen and notepad smoked.

"My characters may come from my imagination, but they are real. No method. Inexplicable. Just is. Just happens."

"Try to explain it—you are what—a biographer, a reporter?"

"I guess you could *say* reporter. Yes, you could say that."

"What I say is not important. The key thing is what you say." He scribbled more.

"I just listen to them and write down what they tell me."

"So—you are *positive* they are *real*?"

"Yes, of course they are real. I wouldn't be paying you to help me relate to them better if they weren't. Anything else would just be crazy."

* * *

MATT BELIEVES WRITING IS EXTREMELY important. He explained to me, "Writing extends the shelf-life of storytelling, which has been our method for culture to exist and thrive by transmitting knowledge and wisdom."

Next to figuring out life, Matt believes writing is the best activity to engage in. He believes the language of fiction is more important than the fiction itself. That's serious stuff.

He often said, "Writers, the new storytellers, observe more things and in greater detail, then they share them with others. Most important to know and remember—always believe the unbelievable. The impossible is possible."

For Matt having a sense of humor was extremely important, too. Right after explaining such important concepts as I have mentioned he dropped this Matt Fact on me, "Did you know that Victor Hugo wrote in the nude?"

And then there's music.

Matt loves music—almost as much as baseball. He is as eclectic and original in his tastes for sound as he is with words. When Matt came in my room his entrance theme was his mimic of Bobby Darin doing *Mack The Knife*. It was Matt's way of announcing he had arrived.

For fun, Matt plays a game of connections with names of artists and songs. He revved up his portable device and start with something like Frankie Lymon and the Teenagers singing *Why Do Fools Fall In Love?*, then Frankie Valli's *Can't Take My Eyes Off Of You*, followed by Frank Sinatra doing *Summerwind,* followed with Billy Stewart's phenomenal *Summertime*, then the Lovin' Spoonful doing *Summer In The City*.

Get the drift—I mean, the connections? After an hour or so of progression through all types of music in that manner, he'd switch to Mozart presented in 432 Hz, playing it as low background to his readings. Sometimes he'd play and sing along with Dean Ford doing *Reflections Of My Life*.

Matt particularly loves the line, "The world is a bad place, a bad place, a terrible place to live. Oh, but I don't wanna die."

Pain. Sorrow. Hope. Matt understands it all, and with him leading me, my mind grew.

Over the years as Matt read to me, there were times I got to the very brink of waking up.

"I know you can hear me," he'd say softly. The love, kindness, and truth in his voice was amazing. "I sense you are coming out of it."

And, then, poof—something would pull me back. I was defeated. I was so very close. So many times. But Matt did not give up.

Within his core, Matt knew I could come back at some time. For him, it was not *if,* but *when.* His attentions sustained me. He never gave up—never abandoned—me. Remember, his belief in my ability to believe got me to Neverland.

I may still be in a coma, but I can flit about and I am always learning.

Matt is *my* mentor—and so much more. I guess there can be a good side to being hit by a rock.

---

* * *

ONE DAY I'LL WAKE UP—AND when I do, I won't be a mentally disabled giant. I just wish I could tell Matt how much I appreciate all he has done for me. Instead of Matt feeling guilty about that rock missing him and hitting me, I'd like him to know I heard him as if I were awake, and that I remember—everything.

More importantly, I want to tell him about my experiences flying through time and space. Experiences—like what I propose now for you and me.

Right now, Jude is in his office at the newspaper. Let's visit him. When we do, I feel there is a chance Matt won't be far off.

* * *

JUDE, THE REPORTER

SOMETIMES, WHEN I'M ZIPPING AROUND flying, I can get inside the thoughts of the principal players in what I call "the drama of my trauma".

For example, I can hear what Jude is thinking. It's as if I am in his mind. Like now, when Jude tells himself, *Peeling back your own skin and peeking underneath is painful. It might even prove dangerous. A lot of the folks in my situation turn to drink. As they say, "Once you know, you cannot un-know."*

For me it is doubly dangerous, as I am already fond of the bottle. Very fond. Too fond. I always placed first in my college-day drinking games. Yeah, way too fond.

In fact, right now my 'brown water' friend is perched on my cluttered desk whispering come-hither. To counter its allure, I focus my gaze at one of the two important items on my desk. The one I am fixed upon is a familiar newspaper clipping. The article has been with me for years. Framed, not one of mine, it incorrectly recounts an event that for some unknown bizarre reason I simply refer to as The Incident.

I have looked at the article often since my uncontrollably upset father waved it about.

"Our family's name and reputation are important in this community. I swear!" he ranted. "Remember, those who tell the stories rule society. If you don't care what people think you will pay a heavy price in your life, because perception is ninety-nine percent of what passes for thought in most people."

That sermonette came moments after he read the account of what happened in the alley. He shoved the paper at me. "You and your friends are seen as nothing more than disgusting little animals." He pointed at the story and shouted, "Here—take a look."

Obediently, I read the headline: ASSAULT ENDS IN TRAGEDY

The account was filled with half-truths and aimed to excite people—even him—one of the higher ranked

perceivers. The article began, "In an alarming dis-
play of criminal behavior a group of local youths, all
pupils of the city's most prestigious private school, are
being investigated for participating in acts described
by police as, 'Barbarism, pure and simple'."

What followed changed my life. Caused me to
become a journalist in a spite-filled attempt to undo
and then outdo the loosie-goosey writing that passed
as professionalism in small town—small time media.
From that day on the article influenced me more than
anything else.

For instance, it led me to where I sit at this
moment.

Here at my desk, I stare at that old clipping and
ignore a photo of me receiving one of my profes-
sion's highest honors. That garbled, misrepresented,
account of that day pushed me—way too far. I had
a crazy idea unbiased articles should be built upon
honest journalism. I was half right. With the recogni-
tion of a big professional prize under my belt I should
have rocketed to a faster track. Instead, I remain
what I am—a small-town small-time timid phony.

"It's a shame," his longtime seductress, Miss
Bottle, purrs, "You deserve so much more. I suggest
you partake of me to soothe your hurt."

Stop trying to seduce me. I'm not going on
another binge. No more Doctor Jekyll and Mister

Jack Daniels. The best place for a temptress is in the drawer. I'll place Miss Bottle there and just say, "No thank you, my lovely. I have to think."

But when I think, I always go back to familiar ground—back to that day. The day described by the local paper. It mislabeled us as delinquents.

We were good kids—just high spirited—yes, just high spirited. The article told of the boy's injury, described the girls' mental trauma, but it missed the most important item. There was no mention of HIM.

I told them he looked retarded but displayed supernatural intelligence. No one believed me. I described a ghost. In their opinion, he did not disappear—he never was. I saw him—the others did, too—but they said he never was.

How do you contend with a ghost that never was? But I've seen him—older—he's still around running errands, showing no signs of being smart. But he's connected to everything that has happened to me since that day. I can't put my finger on it, I just feel it.

When I try to recall that one day, I want to drink. And when I drink, I wonder if all of it ever happened. But it did.

What evidence is there? Kyle Rattigan wore the blood. Convenient evidence for our families. They just explained it away. In the end, Rattigan absorbed what little blame our families could not divert or shoo away into the mist.

Rattigan took the fall. Bad for him—good for the rest of us.

* * *

DON'T CALL ME THAT!

INMATE NUMBER 2573275 MUTTERED FOR about the millionth time, "When I get out of here, I'm gonna find that little freak and fuck him up like no one has ever been fucked up. I'll make that retard pay twice-over for each day of my of life that was wasted in a cell."

Inside his cell, one of the many he has occupied, Kyle repeatedly pounded the wall, muttering, "I'm gonna get him…I'm gonna get him…I'm gonna get him."

When finally exhausted, his rant died for the night.

Exhaustion. Fitful sleep. Dreams morphing into nightmares, back again into dreams—this time, a pleasant dream—one where he tortured that 'tard *for making me into Rat.*

Years ago, as the gang leader, Kyle Rattigan's elemental human need to belong warped into a compulsion to control and dominate, principally through humiliation. He was successful by insulting any and all—doing it for fun—leaving hurting souls behind in a wake of pain.

However, his cruel methods only created a hollowness within—his was a darkened psyche that only wanted—more and more. And, that compulsive want, his unending desire, the darkest of addictions, had been thwarted by a "dwarf retard". Kyle became obsessed by the need to get even.

Rattigan accepted no responsibility for his situation in life. He acknowledged no guilt. Suppressed feelings normally lead to depression, but not so with Rat. He was right. He was always right. In his eyes, the whole world was wrong. He could never accept criticism, never credit others with an idea that possibly might detract from his self-perceived superiority. He saw himself as the heroic leader who was unfairly deposed. A victim. A martyr. And, laughably, a saint.

He could not let go of his delusion of unfair treatment. Disgusted with himself for not doing something about it, Rattigan truly believed he had been wronged. And he *was* going to do something about it. In reality, he was just bright enough to be miserable.

He constantly told himself, and anyone who would listen, "It wasn't fair. He ruined me. I was ambushed—tricked."

Listeners were rare—for good reason—and Rattigan earned a month in solitary confinement for attacking a fellow inmate who offered an opinion counter to his myopic view.

"He's a sneaky bastard dwarf. A freak that blindsided me—set me up to take the blame. I'd never be here if he hadn't suckered me and ruined my life." protested Rattigan. A response had come—but only as a question from his cellmate.

"Couldn't it just be that he bested you and you can't handle it?"

Boom! Pow! Boom!

The source of the innocent question was viciously pummeled and Rattigan earned the aforementioned month in the hole. A month in which he learned nothing at all. Instead, he was further fortified in his victimhood. A self-fulfilling prophecy if there ever was one.

It is laudable to try to find the good in all people, but with Rattigan, there was no good to be found. He was a self-centered one dimensional being—all bad—and he cared for no one. Kyle Rattigan loved only Kyle Rattigan. He believed every person and thing in the world was there for his use. In his eyes, all of creation was meant to serve him. Rat Rattigan was deluded and dangerous, very dangerous. Instead of blaming himself for his incarceration, he placed the blame on the shoulders of an indistinct *them,* who had framed him and continued to rule his life.

In prison, he ignored his defects as they were turned outward as anger and violence. Malcontent. Misfit. People-hater. Sociopath. Psychopath. Take your pick.

The parole board saw him as a menace—he was therefore denied release. Destined to serve a full sentence sitting in prison, Rattigan again saw himself as an innocent victim. He remained in denial and did nothing to improve his situation.

Instead, he soaked in a pernicious self-made stew planning revenge aimed at the target he had missed with a rock.

Matt was the agent of *them.*

* * *

In the Here and Now Now

I F YOU ARE HAVING TROUBLE wrapping your head around my flying, me being there and here, back and forth. No problem—I'll be your guide and describe what's happening as best I can. Just so you know, my out of body flying-thing has a mind of its own and I'm not entirely in control. Sometimes I just show up at a place in time and hangout.

When people are curious, they say, "I'd like to be a fly on the wall."

Right now, you and I are two flies— peeking in again on Jude.

Something is about to happen. I have no idea what it will be, but it must be important since I've never had someone travel with me.

And here you are.

Amazing!

* * *

INITIALLY, JUDE BENEFITED FROM THE Incident by becoming the Alpha male of his realm. No longer Number Two, he was at the top of the gang heap. His voice was obeyed. He appeared strong and in control. But as time moved on, Jude began to have fears, as all leaders do. His fear was based in doubt.

He asked himself, "Did I earn my position? No. Do I owe my place on top to someone other than me? Yes."

Doubt constantly nibbled at his confidence. As a reporter, it increased when he was fed information from an anonymous source, a mysterious benefactor, who fed tips to him. Yet he gobbled it up, enjoyed the success it brought, and then, upon reflection, became uneasy with its influence.

Jude's life became a mixed-bag of sweet and sour. Ordered then messy; good followed by bad followed by good. Successful on one hand, haunted by doubt on the other. His life-force was erratic.

And there was something else.

Since that fateful day, perhaps longer, Jude and his phantom benefactor had been tied together.

Matt knows why, and Jude is just catching on. Woven together. Tied. Linked. Their lives are bonded—no, minted, like a coin. However, they are not two sides of the same coin. Rather, they are crowded together on the good side like twins in the womb. On the other is someone else, and it's not difficult to image who.

All this has made Jude unhappy. He is not his own man. He harbors doubt and his roller-coaster life has led him to excesses, of all sorts. When he is up, he's fine. When down, he seeks relief in the wrong things—for instance, he drinks too much.

Like now.

* * *

JUDE STARES AT THE BOTTLE that seemingly came out of the drawer on its own. He replaces the cap after two swigs, and mutters, "Time to end our date."

Miss Bottle complies and is in the drawer again.

"I need to slow down—maybe even quit." Jude has said the same words many times. The drawer gets kicked shut. Temptation hidden is temptation denied. He sets his attention on the diagram before him—a sketch of how CCTV eyes are aimed at key buildings.

Frustrated, he speaks to the bottle in the drawer. "I make my living through my wit and words, you know." He reaches for the drawer, then halts in mid motion. "Stop seducing me. I told you to stop tempting me. I need to think." Jude rubs his eyes and stares at the diagram.

"I couldn't figure it out," he tells Miss Bottle, "but then I did. All I had to do was connect the dots. Now it's clear. I thought 'whoever he is, I'll find him'. But I found the ugly truth—he's the dog and I'm the tail. Dammit! I hate that I owe him—and there's no way to repay the debt."

Jude succumbs and opens the drawer. He takes a drink.

"I'm such a fraud," he mumbles. "On top of the world 'til I figured out my being there was not due to me. Yes, I'm just a sorry fraud—an ignorant one to boot."

Jude stares at *The Desk*, his desk, the seat of honor where the head reporter sits.

"I thought I had the right to be here. By newsroom tradition only the top-dog can occupy this desk. By rights it is mine. But I deluded myself. I'm a fraud. Just a guy who passed along tips and leads handed to me—the fraud—a follower not a leader. I do not deserve any praise."

Jude retrieves the bottle, pours a triple shot into his coffee mug, and walks to the window. He stares across Queen Street at the new Convention Center—the subject of articles earning him a Pulitzer nomination, and offers a toast.

"Thanks—to all the anonymous sources." He drains the mug.

The convention center story looms in his mind.

What started out as a puff piece on the re-purposing of the old Watt and Shand department store site turned into a series of investigative articles outlining inside deals and incompetent tone-deaf elected officials. In the end the city got an under-utilized hotel stuck behind the façade of the old store, a third-rate meeting site, and plenty of fees, taxes, and assorted costs. What the local Powers That Be got was a string of high price construction contracts, with little or no oversight. The local existing hotels, well out of the range of any conventioneers, were forced into assisting the ongoing funding of the project through a complicated scheme of exorbitantly higher room taxes, which dampened their occupancy rates. The final "screw-the-public" frosting on the cake came in the form of the loss of the historic-site designation for the old store. God only knows what the minuscule county commission got. The monumental project was decided on by only the three members making up that body. Imagine, three people set the course for a population of seven-hundred thousand.

A great series on a story fed to me all the way. Fed by an anonymous source.

We truly are the imaginations of ourselves. I really believed I was an investigative reporter. Instead, I was just a mouse in a maze. A pet mouse—his pet mouse. He took years to build the maze. I only found the cheese when he let me. The source was in charge all along. The cheese was placed before me and all I had to do was write about what I found. Found? Hell, it was put right under my drunken nose. Anyone could have done it. He picked me and fed me his cheese. Why? I can't imagine. But, in my bones I know it's him—Otto Janus, the J. D. Salinger of Amishland—he's got to be my secret helper, the *anonymous source. It fits the M. O. of his life. I'll turn it all around—gonna follow my hunch his failure in staying anonymous was in using that Down Syndrome dwarf to drop off messages.*

Jude looks at the new hotel rising above the building's historic façade and half-laughs, half-says, "I must admit, my readers do love the cheese, and the story behind that place did make great copy."

Returning to his desk, he pulls out a worn scrapbook and continues talking to himself. "Every story with my byline is here. Now, I realize that so many— almost all the good ones—have his imprint. Yep, he placed the cheese and I found it. Everything is just as he wanted. As a plagiarist I used the unknown source's input to play the reporter—to get what I did not deserve. I was stupid to forget he knew all along what I was—a thief."

"What about now?" he asks, staring at a diagram he sketched to depict the situation. "He's become the story. He's the cheese. I know where he is. What he is—fantastic stuff. But, dare I write *his story?* If I do, I tell about the sorriest part of mine. Figuring out who and what he is—connecting the dots—the best, the only real investigation I've done will show me to be a fraud—and a stupid one at that.

"When I think of it, I have written only a few stories of my own. Tips. Leads. Half-written pieces. The rest were all delivered to my door. I took 'em.

Committed outright deception in filing them. I'm so fake. A fake, with a penchant for phantoms—that retard, Mick, who avoids me like the plaque"

He opens the drawer, fondles Miss Bottle, and then sucks her dry.

* * *

ART DOES NOT HAVE TO
MATCH THE COUCH

MYA HAD THE TALENT TO go anywhere—New York, Paris, Florence, Chicago—any-where. Her school was in Philly, an up-and-coming community on the art scene, but it could not hold her. Everyone who saw her work urged her to stay. She was offered many inducements, but she steadfastly declined. After art school, Mya came home.

"I want to live in a community, not just an art community," she told all who really cared to listen. "I don't mean to offend anyone, but artists don't need each other. The good ones work alone," she explained. "We are self-absorbed and crave quiet and solitude to create. When I come up for air and I step outside, I want to be among all types of people, not just other ego-driven personalities. And, please don't get me started about the *prima donnas*." The truthful ones nodded agreement.

Lesser talents, wannabes needing the cradling hands of teaching salaries, fawning for praise and mindless coffee-house chatter, muttered hollow well wishes. Under their breath they said, "You'll starve. You'll be back." A lot of them were *prima donnas*.

They were wrong. Mya flourished and she never looked back.

* * *

AT TIMES MY FLYING-THING IS difficult to control, but I'm getting better at aiming. I practice, and when I do, I try to land on whatever time and place Mya is near. Just *now*, I'm going to Mya's shop on Prince Street.

I feel good whenever I see Mya. Her shop is in the arts district about a block from where Matt lives. I like her shop, SPITALFIELDS' ART EMPORIUM. It's full of her creations—sparkling jewelry, clothes in bright colors, and really beautiful paintings.

* * *

AS AN ARTIST, MYA'S WORK is varied She is adept in many mediums, but it's her brush work that is special. Her work seems alive. The natural glow of flowing, yet, at times, sharply-edged areas of contrast allowing her watercolor selections to move on their own.

"It looks real, because it is," she explained. "A truthful inspiration has its solitary life. An inspiration comes, then goes. Like all of us, it has a life and then a death. With watercolor, you can't hide mistakes."

There is an item in the back of her shop—my favorite—a watercolor she painted near the end of her first year of art school.

Like so many others, Mya and friends took their spring break in Florida. But, rather than party and sun herself on the sand, Mya spent time indoors with an instructor at the Salvador Dali Museum. Inspired by *The Temptation of Saint Anthony*, on loan from its home in Belgium, Mya modernized Dali's spiritual masterpiece using watercolors. With amazing talent, she depicted her vision of the procession of temptations being confronted by a dwarfish figure holding a book rather than a naked Saint Anthony wielding a cross.

It's not hard to figure out who was holding the book.

Many people have tried to buy it, but it's not for sale. She explains to inquiring potential buyers, "Some things must be gifted, or shared—never sold." Mya is resolute. Focused. Principled. Some people would say she is stubborn.

When the local First Friday Committee proposed, actually mandated all the shops and studios in the arts district provide wine and finger-food to the wandering participants as an inducement to boost attendance, Mya balked. She had no problem with fronting the free goodies, she just bucked at being *forced* to do so.

Mya is a free spirit in life and as an artist. Her response to the pressure was to drape the shop's windows in black and post a sign boldly on the door: IF YOU WANT TO SEE SOME WONDERFUL ART, COME BACK TOMORROW.

Curious folks returned. And they bought. Her following began, and then quickly grew. Critics and buyers trek from Philly, and beyond because they like Mya's art.

I like everything about Mya.

Matt does, too.

* * *

I SMELL A RAT

As I FLY, I RECENTLY have seen a dark cloud hovering over parts of the city. Intense. Dark as dark can be. Mobile—as if it has a mind. Everything about it is ominous. I fear what it represents—what it hides. I am afraid.

* * *

RELEASED FROM PRISON, RATTIGAN FUMES and mutters. "Since I've been back, I've looked for him—and not just out of the corner of my eye. I am hunting him. The scummy back stabbing little creep—a fuckin' retard taking up space—breathing air meant for his betters. Me!"

Rattigan spits on the ground. "I saw him for sure—I know it. Yeah, I saw the little fucker down at the Central Market, but he slipped away. I asked around, caught a whiff of information, figured it out. I know who his friends are—where he goes at night."

He spits again. "Let's see how *he* likes to be blindsided. Revenge is best served up cold? Nah, I can do better. My revenge will be a frozen chunk of ice—dropped out of the sky crushing everything he knows and cares for."

* * *

THE DARK CLOUD HAS FOUND places it likes to perch—above an apartment on Water Street, the newspaper office, Mya's art studio, and the Parker Home.

It's a sign—a bad sign. The Rat is out of prison. He's back, and he is near.

I'm no longer afraid—I'm terrified.

* * *

STILL WITH ME? I'LL FILL you in some…the dark cloud has affected everything. Matt missed his visit. I've tried to aim for him, but I have failed.

My mind is clouded by my fear. My aim keeps leaning toward Jude.

I bet if we check on him again, he'll be drinking. He has been at it for days.

* * *

Remembering a Break-In on Water Street

AT HIS DESK, JUDE POURS another drink and announces to the empty office, "Breaking into the apartment on Water Street was just a logical step in my search process. A man's gotta do what a man's gotta do."

He grins and thinks about what may happen should what he did become known. *It would make a great headline: LOCAL REPORTER ARRESTED FOR BREAKING AND ENTERING. A great way to cap off my career in journalism.*

What was I thinking? Whatever it was, I certainly wasn't expecting what I found. I was just back-tracking my source. I should have left well enough alone.

Jude tilts back in his chair, with laced fingers behind his head, he closes his eyes and thinks, *Maybe what happened is a drunken dream.*

* * *

THE APARTMENT SAT ATOP AN old garage on Water Street across from the Hole-in-the-Wall Puppet Theater. During daytime hours, the neighborhood's commercial trade was supported by moderate foot traffic. At night the area was thinly populated and quiet. No one saw Jude climb the stairway to the apartment.

Getting inside was not difficult. The lock was a familiar type. Jude jimmied the door with a simple bump key similar to those he used to burglarize homes in the upscale neighborhoods near Buchanan Park when he ran the gang.

Easy peasy—surprising what skills stay with you. Jude entered the apartment and surveyed the place. *Not what I expected.*

The small living space was immaculate. Three sides of the main room were floor-to-ceiling bookshelves. Along the fourth wall, a day bed sat with a reading area of two chairs and a small table. Two video screens and a computer on a desk defined a workspace in the corner. A single small window overlooked the street. The room's only exposed wall was painted bright white and adorned with eclectic artwork above the bed.

Something's wrong here. I thought I was following the messenger. He's handicapped, a retard actually, and only the go-between. Maybe he doesn't really live here. Yeah, that's it—this must be a worksite or safe-house. Jude moved toward the book shelves. Quite a collection.

Nearly a thousand books were neatly arranged by subject matter. History, science, philosophy, mathematics, art, and music—in English. Then there were sections of Spanish, French, German, Japanese, and Mandarin. Whoever the disabled messenger works for is a serious reader and collector of books.

There's a fair collection of fiction here. He focused upon familiar titles by a local novelist. I see he's fond of the mysterious and reclusive Otto Janus. My hunch gets better and better.

I wish I had come up with his approach for a who-done-it series—an Amish detective—amazing. Great premise. It figures that someone enmeshed within in a closed community could develop exceptional skills at observing human behavior. Set that person loose in the general community and there you have it—a super detective.

Jude's fingers walked lightly across the books' spines.

Janus also has adroitly moved into other genres of fiction—been able to branch out based upon the commercial success of his Rumspringa Mysteries. Popular and evasive—no one has been able to sit

him down for a talk, or even a photo for that matter.
Looks as if my trailing the messenger has paid off. My
bet is that the gnome's boss is Janus himself. I hope
I'm right with my hunch about him being my source.

The reporter in Jude kept searching—eyes and fingers stopped at the same spot on the bookshelf.

"What's this?" he murmured as he pulled a notebook from the shelf.

It appears to be some sort of memoir or journal.

Jude opened the cover and read the opening entry, a familiar poem written in a bold clear hand:

ODE TO UNRECOGNIZED WRITERS

Every morning the task is unfinished
yet toiled over,
our hands arthritic
—they still pound words
to mother, to father,
to God & old friends—
It's a labor
of love,
no promise of riches
would hinder
or maximize
the process—
And the writing remains

when the bones have
turned to dust
whether or not
they are read.

Jude's eyes brightened. *I'd know this anywhere. It's the tribute poem Janus places in all his books. I remember the rare online interview, where he recounted how he paid a street poet, Abigail Mott, five dollars for an impromptu piece that would encourage him to write. Janus shared he starts each day by reading her poem. When his first book was picked up a publisher, he made printing the poem a part of the deal and has continued to do so with every following effort.*

Damn, I've hit the mother lode. I have found him and where he writes. No—I've found where he hides. Nailing an interview with Janus is no longer a goal—with what I know—it's a done deal.

Jude eased into a chair close to the desk, *probably used only for reading.* Within arm's reach were books with multiple pages bookmarked. On the corner of the desk was a signed galley of Stephen Crane's *The Monster.* Also, there was a small statuette.

"The writing of Crane and an Erte piece of art," Jude observed. "Interesting taste—you don't see an Erte just sitting on a desk every day." The other nearby items were a couple pipes, an assortment of tobacco, and a string of Greek worry beads.

He's an expansive reader, an art lover, and pipe smoker—I'd say he's a type B personality—serene, reflective—decidedly passive, non-impulsive. The tobacco is aromatic over the counter stuff, except for one jar marked kinnikinnick. As a reporter, my mind stores all sorts of trivia and I recall that kinni-kinnick is tobacco mixed with herbs, barks, and plant matter—popular with 1800s Plains Indians. It's com-parable to today's aromatic blends. Contemplative thinker, recluse, mystery man of mysteries—a profile piece within investigative journalism—what a story. Jude directed his focus back to the journal.

The opening entry:

The world has the potential to be a very nice place. However, I have found it can be quite ugly. The truth is our brief time on this speck in space is what we decide to make it. We build our one option from infinite possibil-ities. I intend to make my life the best version imaginable. I am determined to find TRUTH. I will be much more than a participant in the game of life. I will design my own game to find the ultimate goal. This journal will be my scorecard and testimony to the power of will guided by good intention, kindness, and respect for the wonder of life.

It seems he had big plans. He certainly met them as a writer, maybe because he has a sizable ego—one big enough to fill the outdoors. It does not fit so well with my tagging him as a reflective thinker.

Jude read on:

When did the game begin—at my conception? Yes, but a serious penalty should have been called on one of the players that day. If my mother had not been raped, I would have been the product of incest. Not a very nice a way to start out in life.

Whoa! This is heavy—dynamite stuff. I see a spectacular interview.

A FAMILY APPEARS UPON THE SCENE
HAND-IN-HAND WITH TROUBLE

THE JOURNAL TOLD A SPELLBINDING tale:

You must go back a long way to make sense of the senseless and I have pieced together the story. Here is what I have found: My family represents all that might be good in Lancaster. And sadly, all that is bad. An epic struggle between good and evil began the moment my first ancestor stepped foot on American soil. As I see it, the struggle was an unfair fight; liquor, money, and sex won.

The dark side of the New World—mostly its unfettered pursuit of material wealth, created an enticement that lured my family ever downward for generations. It's a sad fact, any good my ancestors possessed was consumed by their successes. Chasing and capturing the American Dream destroyed them.

But I am getting ahead of myself—that's the stuff at the end, when I arrive just in time for the worst of everything.

By the time of my birth, the clan was at the end of a long moral decline and was about to hit rock bottom. For someone looking in from the outside, rot was not so easy to see. Cracks in our façade were long in the making. To see them, one just had to know where to look— under the oh-so-proper skin of deceit and decay that thoroughly permeated my family.

Today, the stately family mansion still presides over the intersection of President Avenue and Marietta Pike. It does so with an outward dignity never known within its walls. Successive family fortunes amassed from sly and brilliant business decisions provided the means for its construction and maintenance.

The building is a sight to behold. People passing by are always impressed by its grandeur. Envious of the people inside, they would be surprised to learn the imposing home never contained much happiness. It is a vile a place and I hate it as much as anyone who lived there does, especially my mother. She was driven to insanity within its walls.

'Wealthy and without warmth' is how the clan is described by the people of Lancaster. 'Disgusting' is how the family would have described one another, if they were truthful. As one of them, I know. If I could, I'd hate them all, but I can't. I'm the only one left. I'm the last one standing. Maybe my role is to turn it all around. That might explain why I always try so hard to be good. What irony, I took a long line of sick and greedy bastards to end with me. I am certain they would be infuriated to learn such a damaged specimen represents them. I hope I do a good job not being like them. I believe I have succeeded. Every day I pray I am unlike them more and more. But I digress—back to the family.

The family has been known in Lancaster County for well over two hundred years. Jacob Mueller, the founder, came to Pennsylvania in the late 1700s and made several important decisions within weeks of settling along Conestoga Creek. He renounced his Anabaptist affiliation, anglicized his name, *and began building wagons--Conestoga wagons.*

> *The man known as Jake Miller quickly associated with the less-religious and more fun-loving citizens found in local taverns. It was in these social haunts that Jacob found customers and recruited drivers for the burgeoning freight business he developed. Miller-made wagons were the best of their type and Jake plied them steadily along the Great Wagon Road that led south all the way into Virginia's Shenandoah Valley and beyond. Carrying up to eight tons each, the "stogies" hauled trade goods and tobacco at the rate of one dollar per hundred pounds per hundred miles. Soon Jake Miller's wealth was beyond what he could spend in the friendly taverns of Lancaster.*

Janus related to the Millers? In what way? I thought they all died, or left town. They have disappeared from Lancaster. Jude fetched a cigarette from his shirt pocket, lit it, and returned to the journal.

> *By the beginning of the new century, Jacob Miller was a wealthy man. And thanks to his tavern visits, he was also a hopeless drunkard, totally estranged from his pious roots. His love of drink led him to become a founding member, and then the head of*

Lancaster's fledgling Hell-Fire Club. The club was known to its members as the Dashwood Devils in honor of the movement's English founder. Although the Lancaster branch engaged in milder pastimes than those attributed to its behavioral namesake, the Devils were no slouches when it came to sin. Lewd songs, heavy drinking, and sexual debauchery were the members' favorite activities.

The more devout residents of Lancaster County were alternately appalled and titillated by rumors of orgies, rape, blasphemy, devil worship, and even murder for sport associated with the club. However scandalous in nature, none of the activities were ever substantiated and the group continued to meet in spite of numerous calls for its disbanding—which occurred in 1801 after Jake perished in a foolish alcohol-related accident. He was found below an open window outside his favorite tavern, having mistaken the portal for a door to the stairs. No one was surprised by the incident, as Jacob was often seen drunk in public. Without their leader, the Devils just stopped meeting.

However embarrassing Jake's demise appeared to my family, they rebounded nicely. Jake's eldest son, Joseph inherited his father's business skills and a majority position in the family's holdings. In a brief time through diligence, hard work, and sobriety Joseph doubled the fortune left by Jake. Not to be outdone, his younger brother David continued the family's reputation for debauchery. David was seriously interested in surpassing the legacy of the Dashwood Devils and perfected using the family's financial good fortune to finance his profligate ways.

In the late 1830s David's son, Joshua inherited both his father's inclinations for vice and his Uncle Joseph's fortune. At that time, railroads were being developed and he wisely transferred the family's wealth into the new mode of transportation. It was a brilliant move and paid off well. By 1844, when the Philadelphia and Reading Railroad was first in the nation to deliver more than one million tons of freight in one year, Joshua was one of its largest investors and swam in more than enough money to silence the many critics of his bizarre behavior.

Mid-nineteenth century America, especially conservative Lancaster, was not ready for David's peculiar devotion to nudity and related activities. In the coming years, the rumors of sexual perversion continued as *the Miller fortune grew, and as usual nothing was ever proven. During the 1850s, David purchased a piece of land along Marietta Pike, and it was there that two grand homes were built, razed, and replaced over the next four decades.*

In the 1890s the current structure, now on the National Historical Register, was constructed and it became known as simply as the Miller Mansion. By the 1920s my family's wealth was re-routed through the cork trade and was later firmly placed in another business when the Millers moved successfully again with the trends and invested in an industry that locally produced over eighty percent of the nation's umbrellas.

The reporter-turned-burglar was engrossed in the journal, oblivious to his surroundings, and unaware of being observed. A lone figure had eased into the apartment and from the shadows observed Jude reading.

The darker side of family activities were rekindled during World War II when my grandfather, Russell Miller dumped the umbrella business earnings into war bonds and settled into a long-term project—resurrecting the Dashwood Devils. He was very successful and soon everyone in the region gossiped about how his interests were not just for business. And they weren't. For three decades, my grandfather partied, drank, and screwed at a near-impossible pace.

In shame, my grandmother exiled herself to Florida for its sunshine and her growing addiction to alcohol. When the family's money finally ran out, my granddad sold every asset he owned except the Mansion. At the lowest point, during the second week of July 1975, he sold Candice, his only daughter and my mother, on her sixteen-birthday. Some insiders suggested the old letch had been holding on to her for himself. But he desperately needed money. So, he peddled her to the highest bidder, another hypocritical pervert disguised within a thin-skinned shell of respectability, a closet creep of the worst kind.

"Holy crap," Jude muttered out loud. "What sort of bastard would sell his own daughter?"

From behind, Jude heard a strong and even voice say, "The sick and evil kind."

Jude jumped as if hit by a cattle prod. In midair he twisted about, and shouted, "What the Hell?" landing face-to-face with the source of the voice.

* * *

THE SURPRISING MR. MUELLER

"**I**'D BE FULLY IN MY rights to shoot you, or at least have you arrested."

The owner of the voice stepped forward. Startled, Jude's mouth hung open.

"Am I interrupting you?" asked the voice, laced with sarcasm.

"Uh…uh…uh—"

"Breaking and entering is a no-no, even for reporters."

"You're…the uh…a…the uh—"

"Retard? Is that the word you're searching for?"

"No—no! I mean…I mean—"

"You mean what?"

"I…uh…I…I don't know," Jude said. He slumped downward into the chair and continued staring. Confusion was etched upon his face as he muttered. "I don't know. I don't know. I just don't know." *It's him. It's HIM!* raced across Jude's mind.

"Maybe I should explain." His voice evoked a superior level of command and assurance.

For Jude, the words and their source seemed incongruous. The voice came from a man of about thirty with the distinct characteristics of Down Syndrome.

"You…you…you are just not what I expected."

Matt crossed the room and opened a cabinet. "I understand your surprise. I seldom have an opportunity to present my true self—seldom speak in my natural voice to strangers. But really, at least from my side of things, you are no stranger." Matt continued to speak as he opened a bottle and poured a large portion of its contents into a glass. "Here," he offered to Jude. "I know you want this." It was a popular brand of whiskey. "It's your usual. You better drink it all—fast."

Jude did as he was told. After his last gulp he said, "Please explain. What the hell is going on?"

"You broke into my home."

Jude looked about. "*Your* home?"

"Yes. This is where I live. You should know that. You tracked me here."

"I thought you'd lead me to something…someone else. I've been getting tips for stories from an anonymous source for some time, forever it seems. I thought you were just the delivery man. I…I…had no idea you actually lived here. I thought—crap! I don't know what I was thinking." Jude's expression showed continued confusion.

"It was me. I've been sending you those tips."

Jude stared back in dumbfounded wonder. He was mute. Jude finally broke his silence with, "Why?"

A small laugh. It was Matt's turn at silence. His was controlled. Jude's had been reactive, verging on panic.

After a pause that seemed forever, Matt spoke, "I sent the information for two reasons. I'll start with the state of your profession."

"Journalism?"

"Yes—it stinks."

"How so?"

"The old-fashioned methods and zeal are gone. Real investigation—the kind that was long ago behind the majority of stories in the paper and on TV—has been killed by technology…and laziness. The internet is the unplanned-for-culprit. Good reporting has been replaced by virtual gossip—a form of unstructured unorganized ignorance.

"The media's leadership is the worst. They take good salaries, prestige, and absorb all the ego-boosters they can get from the hands of people not their betters—people who are just better at being wealthier. The real people at the top, who dole out the goodies, do not encourage any sort of real service to society. They have their own private sources of news and communication. They are happy with the profession's decline. It makes it easier for them to stay at the top, even though the base of the pyramid they perch upon is rotting.

"No longer do we have a literate print-based culture, where people handle complex ideas and separate illusion from truth by understanding some basic tools of logic, as opposed to feelings. Social media has some fine uses, but not in creating and egging on image freaks addicted to filling their brains with electronic based images—always needing constant stimuli to get that next fix. The result is that they cannot tell the difference between lies and truth.

"It's sad. Our society has lost its edge. Humans can plan, model, extrapolate, innovate, design, create, build, and, unfortunately, destroy. Also, we can imitate reality, and thereby fool ourselves. Journalists are supposed to stop us from confusing imitations with what is real.

"What irks me the most is the intelligent people in your work, smart but in no way geniuses, think they know so much. And they act so superior displaying what I term as smugnorance—ignoring their failure at knowing while parading a misconceived mental-superiority over *them,* the very people they should be serving. Mark Twain saw it so clearly when he evaluated, 'That awful power, the public opinion of the nation, is created in America by a horde of ignorant, self-complacent simpletons who failed at ditching and shoe-making and fetched up in journalism on their way to the poor house.'"

Matt caught himself ranting and apologized, "Sorry for carrying on, but I needed to get that stuff out."

Jude gave him a nod. "It's fine to be so passionate. But tell me, why? Why do you feed me stories?"

"I see myself as an unwelcomed catalyst—to make you think."

"Me? I'm the wrong guy. I'm really just a simple guy. Believe me—I wanted to be complex, intriguing, mysterious. But at my best, I'm a plain-old middle of the road man," he paused, then added, "with a drinking problem."

"Stay away from the middle of the road—it's for yellow stripes and roadkill." Matt paused. "As to the drinking, if you think about it, you really *are* in control."

The words gave Jude food for thought.

Matt continued. "I did expect you to show up—just not quite so soon. And not by way of a break-in. I figured you would eventually pick up my trail based on the clues I've been leaving. But honestly, I didn't count on you reverting to the petty crime of your adolescence."

Jude shook his head vigorously. "No, this isn't happening. This can't be right." He closed his eyes and shook his head again. When he opened his eyes, he looked directly at Matt and his disbelief slowly changed to wonder, then reluctant acceptance.

"This is not a joke, is it?"

"Depends on how you look at it."

"Damn it! Stop!"

"Stop what?"

"Stop playing with me. Tell me—what the hell is really going on. Who *are* you?"

Matt laughed.

Jude fumed.

"I said, stop it!"

Matt grinned and asked, "Alright, what exactly do you want me to explain?"

"Ah…ah…ah… Damn. I don't know. I don't know." He looked at the empty glass. "I need another drink."

"You sure?"

"Never been so sure in my life."

Matt spoke as he poured. "Okay, but on one condition."

"Yeah, yeah, sure."

"Watch your mouth. Your language annoys me."

Jude appeared to blush slightly. Then he said, "You have to admit—I mean…" He pointed to his host. "One minute I'm hearing a lecture—a good one. And then I am back in reality confronted with you not being—looking …" His voice trailed off.

"Is 'normal' the word you want?"

"No…no…I mean…you don't…don't sound the way you should."

"Because I have Down Syndrome?"

"But…you speak and look like—"

"—like I'm *not retarded*?"

"Yes—no…I mean—No!" Jude looked bewildered. "What the f—" He caught himself. "Sorry. I…I…" He tossed his hands up in a sign of giving up.

"Down Syndrome? How can...do... you... How..."
His voice trailed off.

Jude's expression admitted complete defeat in understanding who was standing before him. The reporter in him prompted him to look at the books lining the walls, the massive computer set-up. "It's safe to bet that all this yours."

"Yes, all mine. No one else lives here."

"Damn!" Jude continued to stare at the array of books.

"I've always loved reading," Matt explained. "I would have kept more books, but my space here is limited. In one sense the internet has been a blessing. Knock technology all you want—social media is screwed up—but the availability of knowledge is almost perfect. But, new tech's flaw is that it nudges out the old tech of books. I love books. Holding knowledge, a book, being tactile with it makes the experience ever so personal. Even the driest of fact-borne knowledge is made more human, approachable, when discovered in a book, as opposed to looking at it a screen.

"As a child I read encyclopedias. Heavy to lug them around. Today, vast collections are available at our fingertips. Sadly, few people are taking advantage of all the knowledge that is available. Ninety five percent of the airtime on mobile phone devices is pure junk—people chatting crap like, 'Hey, this sucks—there's a line at the coffee shop.' It would be nice if more of the usage of our devices increased understanding. Sadly, we are all ignorant, just on difference subjects."

Jude was impressed by the scope and nature of his host's thinking. It led him to look more closely at the titles.

"You read French?"

"*Qui.*"

"Spanish?"

"*Si.*"

"—*and* all the other languages on the shelf?"

"*Jah.*" Matt smiled. "I particularly love German. Did you know that the High German language, with its clear grammatical structures encourages the development of better-connected, more clearly formed neurological circuitry during early childhood?"

Dumbfounded again, Jude mumbled, "It's amazing."

"As a writer I thought you would appreciate that sort of fact. You'll agree—language is indeed the key to knowledge and understanding. The language you speak in, and dream in, wires your hard drive—your brain. It's the software that influences hardware."

Still mumbling, Jude uttered, "This is beyond *anything* I thought I'd find."

"What did you *really* expect?"

"I *really* thought you were just a delivery boy—a go-between. I knew you we smarter than you let on, but not be the mastermind. I believed you'd lead me to the real source for all the help I've been getting on my stories. Along the way I figured it might be Otto Janus and you would lead me to him. You really are him."

"Yes, here I am—Otto Janus. Surprised?"

"This is so way, way, way beyond. Everyone has been trying to find Otto Janus—and you're him."

"Yes—hiding in plain sight."

"You've got to tell me *everything.*" Jude motioned for a re-fill. "Do you mind? I think I'm in for a great story."

The host poured a small amount. "Just a short one—this tale deserves a sober audience."

"This is my last—ever." Jude downed the drink and placed the glass on the desk upside down. "Okay, I'm all ears. Start with your pen name."

The host leaned toward his burglar/guest and spoke slowly and clear. "As you may or may not know, my name is Matthias Emanuel Mueller. Friends call me Matt. Assholes call me Tard...remember?"

Another silence.

At a point when Matt knew Jude was eating a lot of crow, he resumed. "It's my small joke. The first name—Otto—is a palindrome—reads the same from either direction. The last name is representative of deception and also art. Janus is the Roman God of duality, always depicted having two faces, and often associated with theater."

"Yes—the two masks, one smiling and the other frowning. I have to admit it's brilliant."

"In my case it has meaning only if you know the thoughts and the reasoning behind it."

"Meaning?"

"What do you know about Down Syndrome? I mean *really* know."

"Obviously, not much. Please, tell me."

"I'm a rarity."

"I'll fuckin' say." Jude caught himself, placed both hands over his mouth, then mumbled an apology. "Sorry, I...I... Jeez I.... I'm—"

"Let it go." Matt pointed to the journal. "You got this far. You deserve an explanation." He pulled up a chair and sat across from his audience. "Down Syndrome is in the chromosomes. I have the Mosaic variety."

"Mosaic?"

"Yes, mosaic. I have several types of chromosomes. Some are typical, like yours. And some are trisomy twenty-ones, like the usual Down Syndrome person. In my case, I have cell lines that are Down Syndrome in areas related to appearance only. The result is I look like I have Down Syndrome. However, in most other aspects, I do not."

"Most? What aspects do you have?"

"Many with DS have a lot of chronic symptoms and complications." Matt gestured in a roundabout manner over his face and body, saying, "Plus—there is the reality there are some things in America worse than being black."

"I never thought it was possible, but you do have a strong argument. That's a *shitty* hand of cards to be dealt." Jude apologized again. "Sorry."

"In a manner of speaking, 'yes' it is a bad hand. Although most people would say I haven't drawn a very good number in life's lottery, I'm okay with it. Most people avoid me, pity me—some even ridicule me—all because I am different. The truth is I pity them because they are all the same."

"How long—I mean when did you know—when did you realize?"

"Early—very early. I think I became aware of my differences even before I could speak. As unfortunate as my looks might seem to you, the real curse I deal with is my mind."

"Your mind?"

"Yes, if my IQ matched my appearance I might actually fit in somewhere. You know—a simple place for a simple mind."

"Terrible."

"Yes—but it's not totally untenable. Due to the way I look, everyone naturally assumes I am retarded, and their assumptions give me unique opportunities. I'm brighter than most—I use the situation to outsmart potential threats and harassment—and to hide from being treated like a guinea pig or lab rat."

"How smart are you?"

"I've never been officially tested, but it's safe to say I am a genius, and I say that without my ego being involved."

"Why—why haven't you been tested?"

"There you go again, the award-winning reporter missing what was actually said. I repeat, I have never been *officially tested*."

Jude did the dope slap to his forehead and said, "Duh! Okay—so why haven't you been *officially* tested?"

"Some nice folks looked out for me. They recognized how rare my condition is—especially in relation to my talents and intelligence. A few mosaics exist, but in the reverse of me. They have normal appearances with Down Syndrome intelligences. I'm the only one like me—to look the way I do and have normal intelligence."

"But you aren't normal when it comes to intelligence, right?"

"Yes. I blew the top off existing tests administered to me on the sly by my doctor—that's one reason I was hidden. Friendly people were also aware of my family history. They protected me from being tabloid material."

"How did they accomplish that?"

"Simple—they hid me in plain sight."

"Hence your choice of pen name. Care to elaborate with some details?"

"They changed my name—back to the original—Miller became Mueller. And through their connections, they placed me within the plain community—one of the Amish Old Order districts—very discreet, very closed. The plan was that I'd stay with them until I was old enough to be re-introduced into the mainstream under the guise of an independent living program. I did come back, but that part of their plan was short-circuited."

"How?"

"That day in the alley. Everything fell apart the day Kyle Rattigan and his misguided friends—you included—botched a sexual assault. They did not think it wise I be identified with it."

Jude was propelled back to the day he took over the gang from Rattigan. His mind froze and he blacked out.

* * *

AMONG MATT'S MANY POSITIVE TRAITS and abilities is that he cares for people when they least deserve it, and need it most. Much of Jude's life and potential has been wasted. I think at this time Matt is going to do more than just continue to feed news tips and ideas to Jude.

I'm glad my flying-thing brought me here. Matt has been acting a bit peculiar lately, even for him. People think I am just a pile of unconscious meat on a slab. They are wrong.

I remember everything Matt has read to me. I am a mountain of sleeping potential. My brain's abilities have expanded. My Now Me mind works in ways they could never imagine.

Join me as I watch and I listen some more.

* * *

MORE ENLIGHTENING CONVERSATION

JUDE OPENED HIS EYES AND regained awareness of where he was and what had taken him to another place in time.

"That day—it does not seem real."

"So, you forgot?"

"It made no sense then. It makes even less now. You—a key figure in what happened just disappeared—I tried to explain, but no one believed me. After a while I didn't even believe myself. And then there is…is…." Jude's own thoughts stumped him.

"There is—what?" The table had turned.

"I don't know exactly, but…" Jude paused, sighed. "I guess people, the ones who are in charge of things—the doctors, lawyers, Indian chiefs—they just want what they want. Us kids—the ones I hung out with—we were the next in line in their world and screwing up is just a bad side effect of what they wanted. They could and would just fix it. But someone like you, as I described you then, was not within the borders of their fixing. So it—you—the whole thing had to be molded their way. If I saw it another way—true or not—it just could not be. My life since then has been so disjointed. I knew you were there and how you controlled the situation, but I was told to think, believe, and live otherwise. Maybe that's why I'm such a drunk."

Jude caught himself in an uncomfortable reflection. *How easily the routine of sin establishes itself.*

He quickly changed the bend of the light shining on him, and turned attention back on Matt.

Matt let it happen.

"They—your friends—they hid you *again?*"

"Yes—the hubbub quickly died down. I came back, But I missed being channeled into another program. Luckily, a stall at the market became available where the Amish owner had ties to my district. He took me on as a gopher and delivery boy. Since the

Amish finish school at the eighth grade, I was seen as just another kid working at the market."

"Man—you've been through a lot. This is an amazing tale."

"Maybe, brother, you should know more about families, relations—kin." Matt pointed to the journal. "I take it you were at the point where I relate just how contemptible my grandfather was."

"I just made it there when you surprised me." Jude looked at the journal. "Did he really do it—sell your mother?"

"Yes."

"Some family. Reunions must be a bitch."

"Some investigator. You missed the point that I'm the last Miller."

Jude softly slapped his head and smiled. "Pardon me. The cozy warmth and caring of your family must have put me off that fact."

Matt appeared annoyed his guest's sarcasm. "You're not impressing me."

"Sorry. Tell me what happened from the point in your journal where I stopped reading."

After some silence Matt said, "My grandfather drugged my mother during her sixteenth birthday party. Then, for a price, he turned her over to an equally filthy pervert, a lawyer from the biggest firm in town."

"Not, Blackman, Rattigan, and Landis?"

"Yes—none other."

"Shit—my father's firm." Jude apologized for his language. "Sorry about that. Our lives crossing like that caught me off guard."

"They cross more than you'd imagine. Take your father—"

"My father?" Jude looked extremely uncomfortable. "You know about...his..."

"Suicide? Yes—and his embezzling from charity."

Jude blurted in defense, "That was never proven."

"Based on his final act, proof was not needed. His end said it all." Matt leaned forward. Jude retreated.

Matt laughed slightly and said, "Look at me. I ought to know what he did to the organization he was paid to guide and protect. I'm the poster boy for Special Olympics. He was dipping into the local chapter's treasury, and he got caught."

"You can't know. I mean..." Jude slumped in his chair. "What are you saying? You're just..." He slumped more.

"Remember, looks are deceiving. Trust me, I know more than you can imagine."

Jude rebounded. "Okay, so he *might* have done it. That law firm was, and still is, full of intrigue. Just look at the guy your grandfather was dealing with."

Matt made no response.

After a few moments Jude broke the silence with a prompt.

"Go on, I want to hear your story. Tell me, what happened next?"

"You don't want to talk about 'Dear Old Dad?'"

"No—I don't," Jude snapped. "I'd rather find out about you."

"But I wasn't the reason you came here. Remember, Otto Janus?"

Jude thumbed the journal. "But you *are* him—and a better story. Talk to me."

"Okay, but on one condition."

"Which is?"

"Before you leave, we talk about you and your father."

Jude started to object.

Matt cut him off. "It's not negotiable. Consider it the price for hearing my story."

"Okay, it's fine with me. But only when I say I'm ready."

"Just as long as before you go, we talk about Jude Blackman Senior..." Matt smiled, stared directly at his guest and finished with, "...Junior."

Jude squirmed and said, "Okay, it's a deal. Now... tell me about your mother."

* * *

MATT SPOKE AGAIN. "THAT EVIL old bastard drove her mad. Prior to that party she had been Daddy's Little Girl. Then, all at once her world disappeared. He was desperate for cash. A hundred thousand dollars was a lot of money in those days."

"Even for a million—hell, ten million—it's hard to imagine anyone doing what he did."

"Not a big deal…for him. He was an evil self-absorbed pervert. Life was always all about him—his wants—his desires. If he hadn't sold her, he would have deflowered her himself. You have no idea how disgusting the man was." There was a deep sadness in Matt's eyes. "Want more?"

"Go on."

"After a nightmarish bout of doped sex with the monster who paid for her, my mother was left like trash on the doorstep of the mansion. She was 'used goods.' Daddy's Girl was now Daddy's plaything. But the joke was on Daddy. Whatever fantasies were floating around in his sick mind, he was physically incapable of performing any of them. Try as he might, sexual abuse was out of the question. When his opportunity did arrive, he was totally, completely, irrevocably, permanently, impotent. A lifetime of debauchery took its toll and nature had its revenge.

"So, every other form of abuse was heaped upon his daughter. In his sick mind, his daughter was the cause of his current state of disappointment. And therefore, she was the cause of *all* things disappointing. You name it—he did it to her. Beatings. Isolation. Verbal abuse. Neglect. Near starvation. The list is just a list if you have not endured its items.

"And guess what? No one in the community did anything. The signs were clear and undeniable—my mother's disintegrating life—dropping out of school, getting pregnant, drunk, or drugged up. None of it was ever addressed by the people who should have cared and acted on her behalf. School officials, neighbors, the city's elite, the church crowd—no one cared. It was like nothing was amiss. Money and power can do that."

"Wait—you said your grandfather was going poor and getting desperate—what power?"

"Not only his. The fix, so to speak, was in because of who he ran with. Don't act like a naïve rube. He traded my mother to the kind of people who do whatever they like. You know—the kind who let their kids run wild in the *better* neighborhoods."

"I've no idea about that," Jude blurted.

"Is acting dumb the best you can do?"

Jude ignored the question. "It's your family's story not mine."

* * *

WE NEED TO GO. SOMETHING else happened. That something is drawing me away to another time and place—earlier today, I think. Like I explained, my flying-thing works a lot on its own.

Verification of an Unfortunate Diagnosis

U NINTENTIONALLY, I HAVE BECOME A super-natural snoop. Often, I have no idea why I am at a spot until later, when the dots get connected. My knowledge and understanding are due to the interconnectedness of people, but often I do not see it until sometime later. I've never encountered this lady. I mean—I've never snooped on her. Claudia takes care of Matt. She is his doctor.

For some reason I have not been drawn here before. I don't know why. But it will eventually be revealed to me, and I'll know.

* * *

CLAUDIA MARCONI STARED AT THE manila folder in her hand. She sighed and thought, *Everything about him is different—even his medical records. Everyone else's records are electronic. But not him—the situation calls for paper—he insists.*

She faintly smiled. No one was there to see it.

I can hear him say, "I do not want my private information floating around by way of wi-fi and lost in the ether. You can never guarantee my records won't end up in the wrong place, being viewed by someone who has no right to know about me. My life is mine."

As his physician, and friend, I understand why privacy is important to him. However, with his considerable intelligence I hoped he would understand and finally accept some of the advances of technology as a trade-off—better medicine vs. loss of some privacy. I've told him that sooner or later his medical condition would be impossible to hide. After all, he is a walking miracle.

Claudia eyed the file and said aloud to no one, "Maybe now is not that time." She read the test results again. She had read them almost to the point of memorization.

"Matt has a point. News like this should be delivered from records you can hold in your hand. Somehow, bad news tied to a tangible source is less threatening."

The results of Matthias Mueller's latest work-up were less than good. In fact, they were terrible. Claudia was accustomed to giving patients unwelcomed news—it came with the job. But this was different. It was Matt.

Years ago, when Claudia took Matt on as a patient, she accepted the responsibility and its accompanying request for privacy without question. Her mentor, Nick Zenos included the arrangement as part of his personal request that she treat Matt. At that time, Dr. Z was retiring and planned on taking a passive role in everything regarding Matt. He informed her, "It is a total blackout when it comes to sharing information on this patient. Guarding his secret is mandatory."

"Why?"

"You'll understand when you meet him."

That was it. There would be no further explanation—and none was expected. Dr. Zenos was a legend at Lancaster General Hospital and when he made a personal request no one could decline—especially Claudia. More than anyone else who had proceeded through Nick Zenos's residency program, Claudia owed him.

I would never have even made it through med school without his understanding and help. He diagnosed and treated my special form of numeric dyslexia and pushed for my acceptance into med school. Then, he guided me through one of his family medicine residencies. "You have rare people skills," *he reminded me.* "So use all of them with this patient. He will test you, but the experience will change you—he's that special."

And use my skills—boy, have I. Matt is a constant challenge. He's got an IQ off the charts coupled with an encyclopedic memory. He must be the most informed layman in existence, on more topics than can be counted. He questions everything—not to be contrary or difficult—just to know and understand. Admittedly, I am at my best when treating him. And, with each encounter, Matt challenges me to be better than my best. And that is what I need right now.

Claudia pushed the intercom switch to the front desk staff, "Please have Matt Mueller sent to my office."

In a few minutes the door opened and her patient entered. As soon as he crossed the threshold, out of sight of his Uber driver, Matt dropped his 'act' and flashed her a smile.

"How's it going, Doc?" he asked. "You look kinda glum."

I'm not glum, Matt—just concerned," she confessed.

"Bad form."

"What on earth do you mean?"

"Being concerned—it's bad form."

"You're always kidding."

"No—you'll lose your edge." He grinned. "I need you edgy, particularly when you tell me the bad news."

"Bad news—what bad news?"

"Claudia, as my Amish friends say, 'Let's sort out the fly shit from the pepper.' I'm on to you. Come clean. You didn't run all those tests for fun."

"I admit I did have some fear that—"

"Never take counsel of your fears." He grinned again and reached for the folder. She did not move to stop him. After reading the reports he dropped the forced grin and placed the folder back on her desk. "I always knew that one day my interest in teratology would pay off."

She pointed at the folder. "Your condition goes well beyond birth defects."

"I know—I'm well beyond birth."

"Matt, this is no time to make jokes." Nodding toward the folder she said, "I'm a fool to believe you wouldn't figure me out."

"Sorry to punch a hole in your ego, Doc." He paused and asked in seriousness, "What is your considered opinion? I'm not going to spend my allotment of eight-hundred million heart beats, am I?"

She had no reply. Her face said so much.

Matt broke her silence, "You know what's worse than being told you have a few months to live?"

No reply.

"Not being told."

Finally, she spoke. "The facts are clear—and not good. Not good at all. Based on the results, there's not a lot of time. Months is the diagnosis—normally. But in your situation, there are facil—" He cut her off.

"No! I'm not entering *any* facility. No matter what you say about being able to hide my abilities I'm not going into any institution—"

It was her turn to interrupt. "Hiding? I'm suggesting treatment and care in the right setting—where we would treat you *and respect* your uniqueness."

"Sorry, Doc. In your heart you know I can't be in a public facility as the *real* me. I'd be poked, prodded, tested, and re-tested. No institutional setting would respect my privacy. Nor could I live the life

I have so expertly been hiding behind." He pointed again at the folder. "Let's be real. Treatment—is not worth the effort."

Claudia made a move to speak but was cut off again. "I disa—"

He was blunt.

"Don't even try to convince me. My heart is so weak that at best you and a facility might be able to squeeze out a couple extra months—maybe a year. For what? So, I can have a little more time pretending to be Tard?"

"Matt!"

"What?"

"Don't use that name."

"Why not?"

"It is so—so insensitive—crude."

"Doc, I said it, not you. Besides, I have a thick hide. The name won't warp me."

He paced to and fro. When he stopped, he looked at her and said, "Did you know that in some circles teratology is also known as the study of monsters? I know all about Nuckelavees, Squonks, and Wendigos—they make much more interesting boogey men than the run-of-the-mill Hollywood werewolves and vampires."

He started pacing again and smiled as he suggested a course of action. "Doc, just help me enjoy what time I have running about. As I am, I get to maneuver through the world I know. The original deal was you would help hide me out in the open. I'm calling you on that."

She did not reply, to give the matter her total attention. After more than a briefness she spoke.

"Okay, you win." Smiling with concern, she came around from her desk and moved to give him a hug.

He half-heartedly dodged her attempt, allowing her to complete the move with some awkwardness. He kidded, "That's not what I meant by being edgy, Doc. And, by the way, you're not my type—you never rode the short bus."

She replied with a second hug. "I'll shut up—but I'm not just your doctor, I'm also one of your friends."

"Friends don't put friends in institutions."

"Ouch!"

"Sorry—but it's my life we're discussing."

"Okay." She points to the folder. "But, as your doctor, we need a plan. When, and not if, something arises. The question is how best do we postpone the *when* of your situation."

"You and I know that in my 'health situation' mitigation is a pipe dream. The downside of the side effects are too much. They would erode my quality of life to the point where the extra time obtained, if any, would just extend my pain. No thanks."

"So, where does it leave us?"

"Me—not us. Like I said, my plan is to keep on living just as I have—and when the shit hits the much-talked-about fan, I'll find '*my* happy place'."

Claudia tossed up her hands. "Childish nonsense."

"Out of the mouths of babes—Psalm eight, verse two." He assumed an exaggerated demeanor of what the world expected of someone appearing as he did and punctuated his transformation with a huge smile.

"Ugh!" She moaned and hugged him—adding an extra amount of energy. "Matt, you are impossible, but I love you just the same."

Matt responded with a hug in return.

Claudia continued. "Matt, I've been blessed by being your physician—and a member of your inner circle. Me…and the others…we care…deeply. We… we…" She teared up and held back a sniffle. "Shit! There goes all my professionalism—right out the door."

She turned away and leaked out some tears and tried to suppress a sob.

Silence.

Finally, Matt moved behind her. He softly touched her shoulder and said, "Don't get so wound up, Doc. I plan to be irritating you a long time."

When she turned to face him, Matt was gone.

* * *

MATT NEVER GETS MANIC ABOUT anything. But he does have serious concerns when it comes to his privacy. As you have seen, when Matt was a toddler, after his mother disintegrated, a very small group of exceptional caring people who recognized and understood his uniqueness stepped in and took action to protect him. Dr. Z and Father Paul played crucial roles in hiding him within the Amish community.

Claudia, recruited by Dr. Z, became his physician and intellectual foil, joining with Father Paul who filled that role in spiritual matters. All were well aware and supportive of keeping prying eyes and poking fingers away. Within an Old Order Amish district, a closed community of twenty-four families, a home was provided. It was like hiding Moses in the basket.

So, why the Amish?

The prevalence of Down Syndrome is higher with the Plain People, as are many genetic disorders, when coupled with their loving and accepting nature and their isolation, placing Matt with them was perfect. As far as the world was concerned, Matthias Emanuel Mueller was just another member of the Mueller family. He attended an Amish one room schoolhouse, moved through the normal progression of farm chores, and read—a lot. During his childhood, Dr. Z and then Claudia checked on him regularly—in secret.

Upon reaching thirteen Matt asked to change his surroundings. He wanted to live in Lancaster. His desire to return was not based upon any unhappiness, from the community or him. Rather, it was prompted by Matt's voracious reading and the intellectual curiosity it fed.

The plan was that he would reside with a Mennonite family in Lancaster, attending, under cover, a program whose completion would certify him eligible to live independently. All that ended on the day of The Incident, causing Matt to return to the Mueller farm to wait out any repercussions which could reveal his special situation.

This discourse is to again point out his intense concern about privacy. For instance, the plot lines and narratives of his writings, particularly the mystery series, were full of false identities and hiding. Matt was not a particular fan of Elvis Presley, but his short story about *The King* hiding in plain sight is one of Matt's favorite themes. One night, when he was troubled by something that may have exposed who and what he was, he read this one to me.

***

FOREVER THE KING

by Otto Janus

FRUSTRATION AND DISBELIEF OOZED FROM Dwayne Preston's voice as his well-thought-out plea disintegrated into a rambling achy whine. "I can't believe it—just can't believe it," he moaned. "This letter. It's unacceptable—it's just so unacceptable."

The ambitious young reporter produced the referenced document. "Look here," he said pointing to a lone sentence. He advanced his complaint physically, placing the letter before Dr. Karen Meyers, the target of his remarks. "I just can't believe this. You did not explain anything—and it's only *one line*. All it says is, 'The petitioner's request is denied.' That's all—that's it?"

Unmoved, Dr. Meyers replied, "Through my brevity I was merely being polite."

Dwayne dropped the whine and scornfully replied, "Polite? Do you really think that as Medical Examiner you summarily dismissing a citizen's request is polite?"

Dr. Meyers remained calm. "I view such requests as pranks and—"

"Prank?" he blurted. Vigorously waving the letter he insisted, "This is definitely not a prank."

With marked firmness and still quite calm, Dr. Meyers responded, "Mr. Preston, your request was denied as all such requests are denied."

Dwayne countered again, "Then tell me—why? Why won't you test the DNA for a match?"

Dr. Meyers explained the situation from her perspective. "Myriad precedents apply. There are rules… regulations…privacy issues…costs….and most of all…common sense."

Dwayne clenched the letter in an attempt to suppress his anger. He drew in a breath and closed his eyes. After a few moments, still seeking a positive answer, he pressed, "Is that your final response?"

The reply was a firm and simple, "Yes."

"Then—here." Dwayne defiantly tossed the letter on her desk. "I won't accept it."

Reaching for the letter, Dr. Meyers subtly brushed the toggle switch for her office intercom. She clearly and firmly said, "I believe you do not underst—"

"No! You don't understand. You don't know. You just don't know—"

This time it was Dr. Meyers who countered with an interruption, "Trust me, Mr. Preston, you have no comprehension of what I do know. Nor do you in fact understand the situation."

Visibly agitated, the impassioned young man sputtered, "No, no! You—you—you—can't—you can't imagine—the—the—the—"

Dwayne froze.

After a long moment he raised himself upon the balls of his feet, drew in a deep breath and vigorously exhaled. Tense dark energy filled the room. In response, Dr. Meyers remained composed. She held her ground. The potential of escalation passed.

Sensing the initiative had changed, Dwayne assumed a new tack. Softly, and with a smile, he near-whispered, "Dr. Meyers, please excuse my exuberance. I sincerely do not want to cause any sort of problem." Before Dr. Meyers could respond, he continued to advance his position. "Please, just give me a chance to explain why I feel so strongly about this matter."

The doctor's expression softened. Nodding agreement, she motioned for her visitor to take a seat while deftly nudging the volume dial of her intercom. Dwayne, focused on the chair he was soon to occupy, was unaware that his words could be heard by anyone in the outer office or the adjacent conference room. As he eased into the chair, Dr. Meyers told him, "Mr. Preston, the floor is yours. I'll give you two minutes."

"Thank you," Dwayne dryly croaked. He composed himself by clearing his throat. "Haaah—hmmmm," he began slowly. "It's a simple case of a celebrity hiding in plain sight. Take his name—Regis Vernson. He stuck it right there in our faces to taunt us."

"I don't follow you," Dr. Meyers replied. "Make it clearer."

Dwayne nodded. "Okay—okay. He took his father's first name, altered it, and made it his last. Vernon became Vernson. Vern's son...see?"

He paused and looked to Dr. Meyers for a response. Her expression remained fixed. Unfazed, he pressed on. "Okay—okay. Then, he augmented Vern's son with a royal title—Regis. You do know that Regis means 'The King', right?"

Dr. Meyers' demeanor remained fixed.

With a not-so-slight sign of consternation Dwayne pressed on. "It's so simple," he explained. "Vernon's son is the King. As in Elvis—the King of Rock 'n Roll. Regis Vernson is Elvis Presley."

Dr. Meyers sat in silence and remained expressionless.

Dwayne shifted his weight from foot to foot. His gaze toward Dr. Meyers was full of yearning for agreement. None came.

She finally shrugged and flatly said, "So, that's it? A name game is the basis for your request?"

'No, no—there's more—I've got so much more." Dwayne enthusiastically replied. "Please—let me share it."

Dr. Meyers leaned over her desk positioning herself directly above the intercom. Clearly, and slightly louder than in her normal conversational level, she directed Dwayne to, "Tell me everything. Give me *all the reasons* why you believe Regis Vernson's DNA should be tested."

Satisfaction poured from Dwayne's voice, "Yes—yes! Thank you!" Smiling, he reached into his briefcase, produced a plastic bag, and launched into a presentation.

"This bag contains a handkerchief. Correction. It's actually a small scarf. It was used by Elvis during a performance in Las Vegas on March 5th, 1972."

Dwayne gingerly placed the bag on Dr. Meyers' desk. He reverently motioned above the bag as if he were picking up the scarf.

"Elvis perspired heavily when he performed," he explained as he motioned with the imaginary item. "Elvis used the scarf—this scarf—to wipe away his sweat. And then—and then—he tossed it to a woman in the audience." Dwayne made such a move with the imaginary scarf, and proudly announced, "Since the performance was videotaped, I can verify the chain of custody. The provenance for the scarf is airtight. That's why I paid to have the scarf's biological residue extracted and tested." He looked at Dr. Meyers, flashed a huge smile, and said with obvious pride, "I have Elvis Presley's DNA."

Dr. Meyers remained composed. "That's interesting, Mr. Preston. In fact, it's very interesting… to a tabloid."

Dwayne's smile vanished.

"You don't understand," he said with a hint of his whine returning. "This is important. It proves that Vernson is—I mean—was Elvis. Now that is important."

"Perhaps," she replied. "But *you* as an individual have no right—no standing—in this matter." She pointed to the letter. "That is why I, as you phrased it, summarily dismissed your request."

Dwayne's wiring was fried. Exasperated, he pressed on. "But you still don't understand. Regis Vernson hid in plain sight using the cleverest of all disguises. For God's sake, think of it. He was an Elvis impersonator—that's how he pulled off the greatest scam of all time."

Dr. Meyers tried and failed to suppress a small laugh. "Yes, that would be quite clever of him. In fact, it would be genius if what you believe is true."

"*But it is true*." Dwayne almost shouted.

"Perhaps," Dr. Meyers said with conviction. She pointed again to the letter. "But, as I said, you have no standing in *this* matter."

"That's absurd. I'm a *reporter* and it's the story of the century."

"I'm sorry, but you are not a member of his family, not a law enforcement official, nor a representative of the court. You are not a party with valid interest. You have no right to ask for a DNA test. That is why I answered your request as I did."

"But—but—what about the right to know? The public has rights."

"Really?" she countered. "What about Mr. Vernson's rights?"

"His rights?"

"Yes—his right to privacy. In death he still has that right. Even if he was Elvis, which is highly improbable."

"But *he was* Elvis."

"Even if that improbability were true, my answer is the same. There will be no DNA test."

"I won't accept it."

"You'll have to."

"No—you don't understand—this is not over. I'll file an appeal."

"Mr. Preston, *you* do not understand," she forcefully stated, opening the desk drawer and extracting another letter. "This ends the matter for good." She stared at Dwayne.

He recognized her strength and silently looked downward.

She continued. "This is official verification that Mr. Vernson's remains—at my direction—have been cremated."

"What?" Dwayne cried out. "You destroyed the evidence?"

"No, I did my job," she said firmly.

Dwayne collapsed in the chair. "There's nothing to match—nothing," he mumbled.

Allowing reality to sink in, she advised, "You really need to end this. You must move on to something else."

After a long silence he agreed softly, "Yes—yes. I suppose it is over." Defeated, he grabbed the plastic bag. "Dr. Meyers. You'll not be seeing me again."

Dwayne tossed the evidence into the wastebasket, picked up his briefcase, and departed.

After a few moments Dr. Meyers leaned over the intercom, smiled, and announced, "Your secret is safe. And, tossing all professional ethics aside, I have been privileged to assist you in evading scrutiny."

Momentarily a recognizable voice replied from the opened doorway, "Thank you. Thank you very much." It came from an older, grayer, and heavier version of the man once known as The King.

Dr. Meyers burst into laughter. "You definitely do have a delightful sense of humor."

The man grinned and said, "It's about all I have left now that I can no longer hide in the open. The Regis Vernson cover is gone and at my age it would be impossible to try anything like it again. Our reporter friend has ended that. But I have to give him credit for being very good at his job."

"So, what *are* you going to do?"

"Good question. I think it's time I *really* fade away."

Dr. Meyers was struck by the simplicity and sincerity of his comment. "Even now, after all these years that life—the one of celebrity—haunts you."

"Yes, it does. That life was such a burden and not what I really wanted. It never was as good as people imagined it to be. There's only one true king, and I'm not him."

And, she asked again, "And *now*? What will you do?"

He responded with a softer, older, and wiser version of his trademark smile. "I think it's time I follow a verse from my favorite gospel tune."

"What's that?"

"Quiet like, still some day, I'm just going home."

* * *

MATT'S NEED FOR PRIVACY IS so intense he has kept many things to himself. He often sparred with Father Paul, but I doubt they spoke all that much about details related to privacy. Their talks were about spiritual matters. Even me, his perfect sounding board, was not aware of many things about him. Matt's inner circle was just himself and God.

When I travel, I can see and hear just as if I were there for real. Smelling is another issue. In the spirit world my nose is kaput—except for one special location.

For some reason there is one place where I can enjoy an aroma that gives me peace. Most of the time I can't understand a word they speak during their rituals. As they say, "It's all Greek to me."

Come on—I'll take you there. If you like sandal-wood incense, this place is full of it—and pictures, too—they are called icons.

NEAR THE ALTAR

PAUL ALEXIOS HAD SEEN A lot in his long life as the priest for St. George's Hellenic Orthodox Church. As a young man just out of the seminary, he came to the small Greek congregation nestled within the Pennsylvania's predominantly German and Protestant community with an intense optimism and a rock-solid Orthodox faith. His success, based on decades of service, was undeniable. Now, in partial retirement, Father Paul served as the leader of the city's Inter-Faith Fellowship, ministered to the county prison's inmates, and was considered to be the city's voice of reason due to the success of his weekly radio sermons.

He looked at his buzzing phone. The caller ID told him the topic of Matthias was most probably related to the call. *Claudia rarely calls, but each time she has, Matthias was the reason,* he surmised, and immediately connected the call.

Cheerfully, he said, "Hello, Claudia—I hope you are well."

"I'm fine, Father—fine." Her tone said it all. This was a serious call. "I need to share some information."

"It's about Matthias, I assume."

"Correct." She paused. "He's not doing well… physically." She paused again.

"Go on. Please."

"I'm very concerned. His condition has deteriorated."

"How serious is it?"

"Very."

Father Paul's well-established close ties, and strong credibility with the Mennonite-Amish community, had been crucial in securing safety and ensuring privacy for Matt.

The priest zoned out as his thoughts returned to the past. *Of all the people I have met and served during the years of my ministry, Matthias is my favorite—and he's not even a believer as I know them. How many times have we sparred over the fine points of theology? I have to admit I'm at my best when I'm engaged in an intellectual argument with him. He has a way of addressing the ultimate question of life—the existence of God, his nature, purposes, and relationship with humans.*

Matthias, as I still call him, is infuriatingly persistent in his pursuit of spiritual truth. One of his best shots at me was not even a question, but rather a statement, "It is more important to be a simple child of God than a practicing Christian."

After many years of my helping him hide, when Matthias showed up at the church to question the content of one of my radio sermons, I was very surprised—shocked, really. Although I had assisted in placing him among the Amish, I had not seen much of him.

First, as always, there was his physical condition, which totally disguised his true nature. Then his age—how could such a youth know so much? He was maybe thirteen on that memorable day when I entered the church library expecting to meet an adult scholar wrestling with spiritual concerns. Instead, I found a brilliant contrarian theologian residing in an unconventional form. I asked the room's only occupant, "By any chance have you seen a man come through here?"

The answer was pure Matthias. "No, Father. I haven't seen a soul. Have you?"

I am certain that my mouth hung open for a while, and in response to my surprised look he quipped, "Yes, Father—God does work in mysterious ways—I'm Matt Miller. Remember me?"

"Yes—yes, of course. But the last time I saw you, you were a toddler. I'm so glad to see you."

What followed was one of the most interesting conversations I have ever experienced. And it was the beginning of a special friendship. Only later did I realize his ability to ease me into and through his situation was part and parcel to his unique intelligence. In short order, I lost all awareness of the boy heartless and bigoted members my community would deride as Tard.

"I suspect you came here for more than just surprising a local priest."

"Yes—I did. In fact, I had several things in mind."

"I would love to find out what they are."

"I've enjoyed listening to you on the radio." *He paused for a moment for reflection and then said,* "I have observed that people find it really difficult to admit they routinely judge an issue or personality without filling the need to get a basis for their judgment before they spout an opinion. In fact, it rarely comes to their minds one has to have a basis upon which to form an opinion. I wanted to check you out—in person. See for myself what type man-of-the-cloth you really are. After all, I owe you much for what you did."

"Thank you. But I hope your visit is not that you think I might be a wolf in sheep's clothing."

"No. I just want to know what is in the hot dog before I eat it. I want to be certain you are not something more dangerous than a wolf in sheep's attire—I want to be certain you are not a wolf in shepherd's clothing," *he answered with a grin and a wink.*

"Excellent!" *I shouted. I laughed and he joined me. Then, in humility, I added,* "While studying me, just think of this…if I played Mozart really badly, would you blame Mozart? No—blame me. I am ultimately a pale reflection of the one I follow. Any failure is on me."

"You're okay, Father," *he assured me.* "I think I can trust you."

"Thank you." *I said it and meant it. My curiosity was high.* "Did anything else bring you here?"

"Death." *The answer was calmly delivered.*

"Death?" *My curiosity went into overdrive.*

"Yes—simple good ole death."

"Is someone close to you facing—"

He interrupted, "No, it's for me."

"Are you—"

Again, he interrupted. "No—death is just a topic of conversation."

The interruption was a benign form of impatience rather than rudeness. Later, during our many conversations, I would often experience this quirk. His mind was so quick that it verged on telepathy. Often, he would finish a thought or sentence to move on without realizing he had done so.

"That's certainly not a usual topic of interest for one so young."

Matt opened his backpack and withdrew several books. I recognized one of them as a non-canonical gospel. I said, "I do not often see copies of *The Coptic Gospel.*"

"*The Holy Book of the Great Indivisible Spirit* is the correct title," *he informed me.*

"*Yes*—of course—my error."

"From your tone, I surmise that you disapprove of it."

"It's contrary to—"

"Orthodoxy."

"Correct."

"What do you object to?"

"That Jesus is portrayed as Seth, the son of Adam, re-incarnated."

"I can easily understand why an Orthodox priest would have trouble with that item."

"Yes—it is heresy."

"But isn't Orthodoxy defined by the heresies that form its border?"

"I suppose you could see it that way. But, for us, it's even larger. Take for example the question of who, or what, is God? In the Orthodox view we address it not from what he is, but rather from what he is not."

"What if we passed over the re-incarnation thing for now, and dealt only with his mission?"

"Go on."

"What if his gospel—God's Good News—only said Jesus came to release people's souls from the evil prison that is creation?"

"Yes—I see. Perhaps I could accept it as a treatise on the conquering of sin and death."

"Then there is value—some truth—in that gospel?"

"Perhaps," *I admitted. Finding myself uncomfortable with that admission, I returned to the original topic.* "Tell me—is death really what concerns you?"

"No—no. I am interested in life, of course. It is far more important. But since death is our end, and was your latest sermon's topic, I thought it would be the appropriate topic for this encounter." *Before I could respond he continued.*

"Father, did you know that the world-wide death rate is one-point-seven-eight people per second?"

"No. I was not aware of the exact number."

"Death is everywhere—it makes one wonder."

"About?"

"Why does God bother?" *Matthias asked.*

"Bother?"

"Yes—with death. Why bother with death. In your sermon you spoke of the promise of heaven—a second life—being so much better than this one. Why not skip death and just make this life a perfect one? After all he is God."

"Well…" *I hesitated. I knew I was not addressing a usual layman's concerns.* "To re-use your previous statement—God indeed does work in mysterious ways. His ways are mysterious to us because we, as finite beings, cannot fathom his infinite nature, and therefore his—" *I was interrupted.*

"It's been done," *he said with certainty.* "But, of course, people miss not only where and when, they fail to understand it at all."

"Pardon?" *I was not certain where he was going…or coming from.*

"The Book of Job."

"Yes—yes, of course. I'm familiar with—"

Matthias proceeded with his thoughts, as if I were not there. "After going through all the pain and heartache of losing everything and nearly everyone in his life, Job endures the erroneous and often lame reasoning of his friends only to be confronted by God telling him that he's insufficiently equipped to handle God's view on things. In effect he's told to 'shut up and take what I give you.' Job is supposed to proceed on faith."

"But his faith was rewarded."

"Not very fair."

"What?"

"For the ones who died. Remember—God took the lives of Job's servants and his children."

"Ah! Not so. It was Lucifer who did it." *I was found to be attempting to defend and apologize for God. I am certain that anyone else would have reveled in my embarrassment. Not so with Matthias.*

"The answer is at the end of the story, Padre. Most readers miss it because they focus on God's rebuke of Job for not being present when he performed the acts of creation. The answer is in numbers."

"Numbers? The fourth book of *The Old Testament?*" *I was confused.*

"No, the numbers—not the book *Numbers.*"

I had no idea where he was leading me. My interest was keen.

Matthias continued. "Just add up the rewards for Job's faithfulness. God doubles them all—the servants, sheep, goats—everything is doubled. And, if you follow the theme of your own sermon, even the number of his children is doubled."

"I don't think so. The children are only replaced." *I was certain of that point.*

"No," *he insisted,* "the children are doubled. People miss what is hiding in plain sight. There is a new set of heirs—the ones people see as the new ones—they are the doubling because the originals are to be found in heaven. There are two sets of children—that's doubling."

"Okay—you have a point—a very good point. And it is wonderful because there is a heaven. Plus, the important part of *The Book of Job* is that God was not responsible—all the trouble experienced by Job was initiated by Lucifer."

"Same thing—God and Satan—or Lucifer, whatever is used as the name du jour for the highest of the fallen angels, the Evil One. He and God, as often portrayed in *The Bible,* are basically one in the same. It's his game—all the way."

"Preposterous…" *I again was a defender of the faith.*

"If God is almighty, the creator of all things—he has to be responsible."

"But Satan—rather, this evil, is a product of free will. God's creation of free will—"

"…made it so."

Matthias had hijacked my thought. And then He continued with a point that challenged me— and still does today. "For his own reasons, God applies the notion that at times the innocent must pay for sinners."

"That is too simplistic."

"Not so. It explains the paradox of good and evil," *he said.*

"I guess…explain your view."

"It addresses—and answers—the mystery of God as the creator, sustainer of life, also being the author of death. Father, your sermon about the reward of heaven only makes sense if my point is true. God has to fill in the loophole he created with free will."

"You've lost me there."

"In your Orthodox theology death is the punishment for sin, right?"

"Yes." *I feared we were going to a place that would be very uncomfortable.*

"And, sin is the application of free will in actions not aligned with God."

"Correct."

"So, the promise of a second life—heaven as it is called—is simply a Mulligan."

"A what?" *I still was confused. This lad was besting me.*

"A Mulligan. In golf, a Mulligan is a do-over. God gives you a Mulligan. Job got his Mulligan here on earth. He thought he was God's Number One, but he was not perfect. His sins were covered by someone innocent—his kids and employees. He gets a do-over, the Mulligan, but someone else pays. To make it fair, God whisks them to heaven. It's not apparent, but all is made good by the payors being in heaven. For Job, who represents us all, he gets his reward by doubling all he had and lost. Unfortunately, our reward must wait on us getting to heaven—that's if it really does exist."

"You have doubts, I see."

"Yes and No. I'm searching. I just want to learn more than I know."

"And, Matthias, what do you know?" *This really interested me.*

"I know two things—there is a God, and I am not him. And you—what about you?"

"I have my faith." *At that point, I was thankful for Matthias, for who and what he was—searcher, clarifier, a sharpening stone for people like me.*

"What does your faith do for you?"

"It gets me through each day." *It was all I could say, but it was enough.*

Gesturing to himself—his appearance—Matthias asked, "But would it be enough to handle this?"

I was awe struck by his honest exposure of what motivated this visit. It was evident that his quest—to know the mystery of God—was based upon a burning need to answer the question, 'Why am I here?' Especially important for him was the very personal question of, 'Why was I made this way?'

My answer was insufficient. "Our burdens are never the same."

"Meaning that some get off easy?" *He phrased it as both a question and a statement.*

"But we are all equal in God's sight...and we each have his promise of heaven."

"Words, Father—just words." *He seemed defiant—testing me.*

"Maybe to you, but that is my belief—and it is what I base my ministry upon. I am what I am because the great I Aм made me in his image." *I immediately thought I may have hurt him with a reference to appearance. I quickly added,* "By image, I mean our essence, our soul, is like him. He gave our spiritual form—the real us—free will, choice. God doesn't care about our mortal earthly form." *Again, I had inadvertently touched on appearance. Matthias handled it well. But I felt a fool.*

"Obviously." *Matthias said with a sincerity based upon his sufferings. He then added,* "If what you say is true, it is of some comfort. If not, you at least gave God a Mulligan and that is enough for me. You definitely are not a wolf in shepherd's garb—not like one of those spiritual thieves on TV. I like that you are open to possibilities—like the examination of God and his nature as the creator of all things—and like me needling you." *His smile was sincere and, for me, personally reassuring.* "Father, I might not agree with you on my quest to figure God out, but I do think I can trust you."

I told him, "Sometimes God uses a crooked stick to draw a straight line. I am pleased to know you trust me."

I was truly pleased. And I felt uplifted throughout my entire being in a manner that can only be described as beyond spiritual. Since then, I have felt that uplifting only when I am with Matthias. Knowing him has immensely enriched my life and I'm honored to be one of the people he trusts.

Matthias has revealed his true self to only a handful of people. For years we have fenced and dueled over points of theology, philosophy, and morals. Rarely have I won an argument. And, I have never even been near at winning him over to becoming a member of my flock. Matthias's path of spirituality is elsewhere aimed. It is also motivated with an intensity I have never seen, or even heard of. In Greek there is a word, kapsoura, that describes the burning desire one has for another. Matthias's kapsoura is not for another. His is for truth and it produces refined beliefs purer than I have ever imagined—beliefs of a unique human being.

Indeed, Matthias is a rarity, a positive deviant, unlike most people whose thinking stops at the very point where it should be most intense, which is where their thoughts relate to great questions of destiny.

I recall on one painful occasion he exposed—no eviscerated—my devotion to tradition so completely it occupies my mind to this day. It came when I invited him to explore the mysteries of my Orthodox faith.

"I would be pleased to see you attending the Liturgy," I said.

"No thank you," Matthias firmly replied. "I'm not into organized spirituality."

"But, why? You seem so open—why not give it a try?"

"Too much tradition."

"There's much to say in favor of it."

He grinned and said, "No way. I think that organized religion kills the very openness I just praised you for. I have no respect for church tradition."

"Please tell me why."

"Simply, within a few short years after Jesus left—and I'm not saying he ascended anywhere—his followers altered his wonderful teachings. They set up an organization instead of doing what they were told to do.

"They were to emanate love so those who are in need, the broken-hearted, the lost or unloved, the homeless could trust them to care in the same manner the Good Samaritan forgot cultural differences and aided the injured man he found lying in the roadway. Instead, the higher ups weaseled out of the sort of humble benign leaders who washed feet. Instead, they told underlings to set up structures to do the real work while they attended to stuff they thought up as being 'more important.' Check it out in the Book of Acts. I don't recall the chapter and verse because I do not worship the Bible and rattle of such mindless dribble saying, yada yada yada. People who do that miss the essence while they are displaying knowledge on the level of quoting the numbers in a phone log.

"The first people who followed Jesus were simply called Followers of the Way of Jesus, or just Followers of the Way. Somewhere they got off the path. And twenty centuries later you've got cash-hungry con men constantly asking for seed money on TV, as they buy luxury jets, or worse are diddling kids. Religion is toxic. When it comes to structures and the soul, less is definitely more.

"Roll this about in your head for a while. Imagine you have a cage with five monkeys inside and hanging on a string above a staircase in the middle of the cage you have a banana. One monkey will eventually try to climb the stairs to grab the banana, and when that monkey touches the stairs, spray the other monkeys with ice cold water—really freezing water—give 'em a healthy blast. Then wait.

"After they recover, another one will attempt to grab the fruit. Repeat the blast. Again, after recovery, the spraying is repeated when any monkey touches the stairs. Then you have a bunch of cold wet monkeys who prevent any in the group from even approaching the stairs. The fruit, no matter how tempting is off limits.

"Now, stop the spraying and replace one of the monkeys with a new one. When the replacement monkey sees the banana and makes his move, the other monkeys will assault him. At every try, he learns the banana and the stairs are in a no-go zone.

"Next, remove one of the original monkeys and pop in another newbie. When the second replacement moves for the fruit, he will be attacked and the first replacement, having learned his lesson, joins in—even though he has not been doused with an ice bath. Then, replace a third original monkey—and the same result occurs. Do it again to number four, get your result, and then do the same routine for number five. The assaults will occur even though none of the monkeys have been sprayed. No monkey will ever again head toward the stairs and the stairway to the banana.

"They act without thinking. They act the way they do because that is the way it has always been. And that is organized religion—tradition—believing without thinking. Father, the lens of your faith is flawed if it is based within a context—the realm—of tradition. I see well-intended, but deluded, people being infatuated with colorful wrapping paper while ignoring the gift."

I have been chewing on that for years, particularly when I don my traditional clerical garments to conduct an age-old liturgy steeped in tradition. I may not agree with him, but Matthias challenges my thinking, and my faith. He has kept me striving to be my best.

Father Paul's reverie disappeared. He had been thinking for what seemed hours—reliving the encounter with Matt—but in reality, it was an instantaneous immersion into The World According to Matthias. Upon hearing Claudia's voice, he focused back on her and the conversation.

"Pardon me for wandering, Claudia. Matthias is a subject that affects me in peculiar ways."

"Tell me about it," she quipped. "As we both know, Matt is extremely headstrong. I think you may be the only person he will actually listen to. That's why I called. I am very concerned."

Father Paul looked at the note. It read: I NEED TO TALK WITH YOU.

"Claudia, don't worry. I believe I have it covered. From what I surmise, I'll be seeing him soon."

"Good, when you do, I suggest you observe him closely." Her concern was real, but only professional. There was no tension in her voice.

"Anything specific I should be looking for?"

"No—just be aware of his overall demeanor. He's had some bad news and he may want to open up."

"Claudia, I'm certain he'll be in control. Matthias is always on top of things. And I have found him totally candid—always."

"I hope so. He may be pretending the news is not affecting him."

"When it comes to Matthias, he is not pretending to be someone else. He's pretending to be exactly what he is—a smart, aware, observant, and caring individual engaged with life. It's us, society, pushing for him to be what we see."

"He is fortunate to have you as his friend, Father."

"I'm the fortunate one. Matthias sees deeper meanings and understands hidden connections. What we see in one dimension, he sees in five-D, or maybe even six-D."

* * *

WHEN YOU AND I WERE watching over Father Paul's shoulder, it reminded me about something I wanted to share. It has to do with what I have experienced by traveling in space and time.

Did you know we humans comprehend time as being linear and sequential? But we do not see it that way in our dreams and memory.

We do not remember time, we remember moments. Like Father Paul does.

* * *

FATHER PAUL RE-ENTERED HIS REVERIE to remember moments with the remarkable soul he knew as Matthias. Such moments as when Matthias commented on the Bible, "Belief was there before the book."

Or, his mirthfulness concerning theology, "Popeye and Jesus almost said the same line. Jesus said, 'I am the I am.' Popeye said, 'I yam what I yam." And, 'Knowing no two snowflakes are alike makes you want to believe in something."

Plus, his very best, showing his understanding, respect, and love for others, "Ubuntu is a Zulu word, it describes relationships beyond the concept of democracy. It means, 'I am because you are.'"

I am so grateful I know him. When Matthias meets God face-to-face it will be interesting—the odds might be even.

* * *

Watching Someone Beautiful

As I SHARED WITH YOU, I like everything about Mya. Sometimes she dresses like an artist. Sometimes she dresses the way people believe an artist should dress.

Yesterday, Mya was in the shop all day wearing yoga pants and a man's oxford shirt with the sleeves rolled up to her elbows. Her accessories included earrings that matched her bracelets and a tiger striped matching scarf and headband. Two large Murano glass rings adorned each hand. Her eyes were done up Cleopatra style. Tourists love her look—they want what they want.

Today, she is in her studio working in her Mya look, a t-shirt and baggy jeans with random paint smears. The t-shirt says: FUCK! (ARE YOU OFFENDED?) HOPE AND LOVE ARE ALSO FOUR-LETTER WORDS (SUPPORT THE 1ST AMENDMENT).

No bracelets, earrings, scarves, or makeup.

She's a mess but pulls it off better than any high-paid experienced runway model.

* * *

IN HER STUDIO, MYA IS working on several pieces inspired by photos. All but one is of the Special Olympics. She intends to display them at a charity event in Philly. The one odd piece, done in oil is from a rare pic of Matt—maybe the only one. Matt avoids cameras as if they are radioactive. He's even more camera shy than the Amish.

One day, Mya snuck a camera in her shop and took the pic when Matt was distracted by Miami, Mya's assistant. Miami's real name is Emily. She got the name as a kid when she confused how her Mom referred to her as 'my Emmy'. The phrase got mixed up in little Em's mind. Miami is still confused—about many things. She still thinks she is named after a city…or does she think the city was named for her?

Miami works in the front of the shop on Mya's studio days and when it is slow. Today it is super slow—so slow Mya closed the shop early and has Miami on gopher duty, as well as being a friendly ear for Mya's nagging concerns about being watched.

Miami always listens. It was part of her paying total attention to everything Mya said, did, and wore. Miami wants to be like 'just like' Mya. That's why she mimics Mya's look. Today, she also is in a t-shirt and jeans. Her shirt says: BEEN THERE, DONE THAT,

GOT THE T SHIRT—I'M GOING TO PUT IT IN THE WASH
AND GIVE IT TO THE SALVATION ARMY.

"You know, I just feel it," Mya explains about her
nagging fear. "I've recently had vague awareness I
am being watched. I'm getting a bit jumpy—I know
it—but I can't shake the feeling."

"That is so creepy. How many watchers? Good
or bad? Day? Night? All the time? On special occasions? In specific locations? Any messages? How
about sounds? Any knocking, or tapping?"

Miami always asks Mya a lot of questions. It's
her method of expanding the database supporting her
mimicking. She wants more details, so her 'what an
artist looks like version of Mya' is as exact as possible. Miami is totally blank to the notion hypocrisy is
displayed by wearing the uniform of nonconformity.
No matter how hard she tries her artist look, it is at
its core the look of ultimate conformist behavior.
Unauthentic.

"I'm not certain about anything—just that I feel
watched," Mya tells her. "On several occasions, I
thought I saw someone lurking, but I may have
imagined it, yet the feeling is very strong—won't
go away."

"Say, why don't we smoke a joint, sip some *pinot
noir*, and explore what this means." Miami thinks
it's a vital part of an artist's style to "be mellow".

"Maybe later—I've got to finish the last of the show entries."

Miami is disappointed. She likes sipping, toking, and hanging with Mya, her ideal.

Mya focuses on her work. Concentrating on her art soothes the fear and anxiety within her. Absorbed in the act of creation, she is unaware her fear, in human form, is nearby focusing on several things darker and more potent than *pinot noir*.

* * *

IN THE ALLEY, RAT RATTIGAN nurses a bottle of cheap whiskey and watches the back entrance to the shop.

Closed for the day—the front entry is covered—no one will come in that way. This alley is now the in-out point. Maybe that fuckin' little retard shows up—maybe he won't. I miss him at every place I figure he'll visit. He has a sixth sense and dodges me like he has fuckin' radar. I'll give it awhile and then wander over to that lame-ass job I have at that lamer-ass Parker Home. Good thing stupid people run that garbage pit. I guess they get what they pay for—buck an hour above minimum. I work for shit-wages. The greedy bastards hired me and don't have a clue I have a record. I was told they never dig deep—no background checks. What the hell, on the late shift I can do whatever I want.

He has been there a long time, and he is getting bored. Perhaps boredom is in itself the absolute evil. Drunk and bored, a burning sensation of revenge rises within him. Dark energy exudes his every pore.

I'll make that retard squirm. I'll ruin his life. And his cutesy little girlfriend? She's gonna play a BIG role in me bringing him pain.

* * *

Salami Man

OH, NO! I CAN FEEL it—the darkness. When a terrible thing is about to happen, I get nauseous—really sick. I'm always alone in the Parker Home when the bad ones come to visit me. I don't want you to be here.

When the bad ones are around, I hide. I go away. Flying is a blessing. The first time they came, I just froze and remained with my body.

Since then, I have learned it's best to fly away and protect myself by visiting nice places. I see the Lost Boys. While I hide on their island, I share with them what Matt has read to me.

The boys show a lot of interest, but I think they'd rather have me teach them to fly. For some reason, Peter has never sprinkled them with fairy dust. Maybe underneath they are jealous. No matter. By being with them, recalling good memories, I am able to block out how the bad ones treat me.

I hope you cannot see what they do. It is painful for me.

* * *

"**Y**OU READY?" ASKED RATTIGAN. HE checked to see if anyone was near.

"Yeah, I'm set," his companion almost shouted.

"Shhh! We need to keep it down."

"Okay, sure."

Rattigan lifted the sheet, and in a whisper, he said, "See? Didn't I guarantee the product? A cock that big is hard to find."

His companion was silent. The woman's eyes remained focused on the crotch.

"You weren't lying—it's enormous."

"Like I said, it's the biggest snake in the state—and it's all yours." He thrust his hand toward her. "Time to pay up."

The woman gave a small, embarrassed laugh. "Hee...hee…"

"It's three hundred for fifteen minutes."

The woman did not move. Her eyes were fixed.

Rattigan pressed for the money. "There's no backing out. A deal is a deal." He put his hand out again. "Play time is now. What's your problem?"

"Nothing. I mean…are you going to stay?"

"Whatever you want. Hey, I'm not into watching, but if you need an audience…"

"Audience? What sort of perv do you take me for?"

"You brought it up."

"I'm just concerned about…what if he…he… You know—wakes up?"

"Don't worry, it ain't gonna happen."

"How do you know?"

"Trust me, I know. He's been out to the world for years."

"Okay, but you'll stay close? Like, maybe, right outside?"

"Fine. I'll be on the other side of the door. But— where's the green?"

She reached into her purse and pulled out a wad of bills. "Here. Take it."

Rattigan snatched the money, counted, and stuffed it into his pocket. Out of that same pocket he pulled a gold-plated case from his jacket.

"I've got something to ensure you're cool with the experience." He opened the case and extracted a dark home-rolled-looking cigarette.

"What's that?"

"Thai Stick."

"Thai Stick?"

"Weed soaked in opium." He pushed it her way. "Try a hit."

She took it, lit up, and sucked in.

"Whoa—this is nice." She offered the home-rolled back to him. He declined.

"I'm good. Consider it a bonus—for a future repeat customer." He made for the door. "Like I said, I'll be outside. You've got fifteen minutes—have fun."

The woman was disrobing before the door closed.

* * *

IF YOU ARE STILL THERE, I'd appreciate your leaving. Please!

* * *

THE CONVERSATION – PART TWO

JUDE SHIFTED THE ENCOUNTER'S DYNAMIC by leaning forward to encourage his host to continue the story in the journal. "You were about to tell me what happened to your mother. Also, I'd like you to explain how naïve I am."

Matt assumed the countenance of a Japanese *sensei* and began, "She became a captive in our house. Her pregnancy had to be hid. Hiding it was my grandfather's plan."

"I take it that the pregnancy went full term and the child was…"

"Me. And as I said, I am the last in my celebrated family."

"Your mother…how did she…you know… end up?"

"Eventually, as they say, she went off the deep end. She found every pill in the house and washed them down with vodka. She never woke up. My grandfather covered everything up. He used all his remaining clout. He knew where a lot of bones were dumped. Plus, the alcoholic pervert serving as the Medical Examiner was his golf partner. Evil people know each other." Matt sighed deeply. He waited before continuing. "But I'm getting ahead of myself."

"Did your grandmother raise you? Where did she fit in? She was—"

Matt interrupted. "—very tan and very drunk, in Florida."

"Escapism?"

"Of the worst kind. She knew what she was getting into when she married. But what went on drove her into a bottle. Some people react that way. They run away through the cork." Matt paused to look at Jude's empty glass.

Jude looked away, looked back, pushed the glass to the side, and said, "Point taken. Go on."

"In the early days of their marriage, my grandmother turned a blind eye to my grandfather's antics, but the antics accelerated and accumulated. It became too much for her. The incident with my mother was the breaking point. She drank herself to death in record time."

"You said no one in the community acted on your mother's behalf—yours also?"

"There were two—a doctor and a priest. They did the right thing and rescued a scorned and rejected waif later known as Tard."

"Look—I'm sorry about that—the name, I mean. I didn't start it."

"I was there. Remember?"

"That had to be maybe ten-twelve years after what happened to your mother, right?"

"Yes."

"Do you remember what it was like during those intervening years?"

"It was bad, then good—for me. The good people I mentioned got wind of the situation and I was placed with the Amish, remember?"

"I really can't imagine—tell me about that time."

"Like I said, dear old Granddad had a plan to deflower his daughter and then screw her as much and as often as possible. But his lack of cash created a small wrinkle. He was willing to give up the first part of the plan in order to keep his sick ass out of jail and the limelight—but I was a huge wrinkle. A sex slave is one thing—dragging a baby along, another. Toss in my condition and you have enough to push even my lunatic grandfather over the edge."

"He got worse?"

"Much worse. Made my mother's life a living hell. The old man placed walls around her. He was at her every day. Almost no one entered the house and he seldom left. It was as if her status as an unwed mother was license for his behavior."

"What about you?"

"I was initially ignored by him. I was impossible for him to accept. No amount of power, money, or influence could alter my condition, so he pretended I did not exist. My mother immediately picked up on my peculiar traits, and in a way I, was her salvation—at least 'til she could no longer take it."

"Salvation?"

"Maybe that's a bit strong. Her devotion to me was so pure and positive, it created a refuge from the sordid web she was held in. She doted on me. In contrast to her situation, I had a perfect parent—at least when she was herself. Like many abused people she found protection in creating a delusional world."

"You said the abuse aimed at her was daily."

"Pretty much."

"How did he manage to pull it off? I mean making her a prisoner in her own home."

"She was not much more than a child who had experienced devastating trauma. She was a basket case. Even though he was the cause, by the time she was through it her memory and awareness of everything was skewed. For three years he held an extremely tight grip on her. Her daddy was her molester and protector. It was a Stockholm Syndrome situation. Like I said, he controlled her. She never saw the outside of that house—even after he died."

"When was that?"

"A little more than three years after I was born."

"What happened?"

"Family tradition prevailed."

"Huh?"

Matt whistled and motioned in a downward arc. "He took a header down the main staircase—broke his neck."

"Drunk?

"Of course."

"Then things got better for you, right?"

"Not really. My mother's twentieth birthday was the precipitator of the binge that ended the old man's reign of terror, but another oppressor soon took his place."

"Who was that?"

"Your father, Jude Blackman Senior."

Dead silence.

* * *

I THINK YOU FLYING ALONG WITH me has helped reveal much. Learning how cruelly people treat one another, even their own flesh and blood helps me understand Matt much more.

What is amazing to me is that in his pain he has not been engulfed by revenge. Rather, he is a firm proponent of living within calmness, charity, compassion, and love.

Consider how he treats me.

And, then there is Jude.

* * *

JUDE'S MIND STOPPED YET SWIRLED in a frenzy. It splintered, rejoined, splintered repeatedly in light-speed. Silence roared and stopped time pressing its way to forever. Jude thought, or thought he thought. *Father. Shame. Suicide. Rape. Drunkard. Shame, his. Shame, mine. Criminal, him. Loser, me. Genius. Freak. Brother—my brother?* Gears were slipping.

Matt took possession of the silence. Olive branch. Reprieve. A kindness unearned. "It's not so bad—at least you're not me."

A bitch-slap without malice. Matt propelled Jude to a place he had never known. Outside his ego Jude was no longer a boozy, cynical, selfish observer. He abruptly entered the Video Game of Life as a player, not a sit-on-the-sideline-non-participating character.

Jude looked at Matt and no longer saw a list of adjectives. He thought, *we are two sailors in the same lifeboat adrift in an infinite sea. And, he knows the nautical world. Compared to him, I'm just a passenger.*

Blinders off, Jude asked, "How do you do it?"

"Do what?"

"Cope."

"I don't. To just cope is to surrender."

"Maybe, I used the wrong word. With all you have been dealt—you thrive. How?"

Matt was quiet. After a time, he sighed and asked, "You ready for a rant?"

"Fire away."

Another pause. Then: "Just look at me. Imagine—all the time—that you are a freak like me. That's where I start. My anger starts skin deep and goes on for a long time. If anyone has a reason to hate life—to hate my creator, it's me. You know some of my story. My anger was based on the sufferings of my mother and myself. I could find no reason, no justification in either case for what I was.

"I became arrogant and believed if I couldn't see a reason for suffering then there must be none. I was at the point where it occurred to me the material world had no regard for my importance. I wanted to rebel. But at what?

"At first, I threw my bricks at a phantom. Then I assaulted God, the idea of a Creator. The effect was the same. I was a single voice screaming into a hurricane. I was in a dark room looking for a black cat that wasn't there. As one philosopher described, I looked into the abyss and the abyss looked back, and it mocked me just by making me. But I was not giving up. Alive, yet staring at death, so to speak, but very alive, and I knew I had to solve my problem if I was to continue living.

"After much thought, examination, and finally desperation, I tried prayer. I don't know exactly why, but I did. There was no Damascus Road experience. No God-like voice, no flash of light, no vision, no visitation by *Him*. I just prayed. And I felt better in trying. I am a finite being seeking to understand the infinite. Sending a message seemed like the right thing to do. Since that first message, my anger and negative feelings toward God, the Infinite, have evaporated.

"Believe me when I say I was as surprised and shocked by this as anyone could imagine. I mean, when I say I was angry with God, I mean I was *angry* angry. Remember, I hated God. Despised Him. Loathed Him for my existence as his scorned and mocked freak.

"He did not intervene and cure me. He did not take away my suffering. I assumed I had a right to understand everything simply because I existed. I was caught up in the importance and arrogance of my own ego. Maybe there's an argument in that. But who do you argue with? If that is so, then you need God if only as your opponent.

"To disbelieve in a creator God just because He doesn't tell you everything you demand to know is beyond arrogant—it's petulant. Accepting Him, having faith in him is better than flailing at a phantom in the dark.

"To accept God is to accept we human beings are not the all-powerful ultimate beings in existence, and we do not know and understand everything. In the end I came to be at peace with the notion that God and existence are one and the same. I am not Him, I'm at best a part of Him. His creation? His imagination? Whatever. But it starts with *Him*. Acknowledging that gives me peace and purpose. It gives me sufficient reason to keep on striving to learn, understand, and discover as much as I can about who he is and what he created—me—and Why. That's my goal, my journey—it's how I cope.

"I may or may not be on the journey my creator wants me to take—I don't know. But I do know it's a journey *I want* to take. I suspect if I succeed, as Novalis said, I will come home 'to Father's house.' Even if I find nothing, I, and all I touch along the way, will be better off if I'm not a bitter selfish fool doing it."

Jude was overwhelmed.

"Geez—and I was just hoping to find Otto Janus. In my life, I'd say 'I need a drink'."

"You need to stop reaching for crutches—get beyond you. What we are experiencing is not a dress rehearsal for life—it's the real thing—and you only get one performance."

* * *

TERRIBLE PLUS TERRIBLE

WHAT HAPPENED TO ME AT the Parker Home is not good. The dark cloud consumed me, and what they did is much worse than the day the rock hit me.

I am made ashamed by them. Cruelty revels in applying evil in dark layers upon innocent victims.

* * *

"**H**OLY JESUS, RATTIGAN! WHAT THE fuck were you thinking?"

Assistant Police Chief, Barry Snader, a former member of Rattigan's gang, and possibly the most corrupt official in the county, was bug-eyed and one shade shy of purple as he pointed with flayed arms at the woman scurrying down the hallway. In mid-act, the drugged-up thrill seeker had been interrupted by Snader and she fled the scene of depravity, half-dressed, and terrified her anonymity was gone.

"Relax, Barry—it's nothing to get worked up about. I've got it under control."

"Under control? You really are crazy. That's the D.A.'s daughter, you idiot."

"I know. So, what's your point?"

"He's not one of us."

"Of course, he isn't. That's why I brought *her* here."

"Our group told you to lay off this type of she-nanigans. They all agreed you cannot use the patients in this facility as your toys. There's too much risk in this sort of thing."

"They're acting like pussies—always wanting to play it safe. You are never going to get the Devils back to what it was if we are always playing it safe. A few smart moves and we could run this town."

"You call this smart?"

"Yes! No! It's better. It's smarter than smart."

"You *are* delusional. We never should have included you in what we do."

"Bull shit—you let me in because I know about what you do. You, and your wienie friends need people like me. I'm old family, know your ways and all about who you really are and what games you play. Besides, on top of all that, I have street cred—I've done time with *real* fuckin' bad dudes. I ain't some wannabe wimpy closet-type like you and your friends."

"But the risk—"

"—is covered. I left a camera hidden in the room and recorded Little Miss Fuck Up getting her perv-on with the meat mummy. Now we own that punk-ass D.A. He is ours—or at least his daughter is, and that's as good or even better than what has been produced by those pussies running your group. I picked her out because I owe her do-gooder daddy some payback. The asshole locked me up, remember?"

Snader relaxed some. "Okay, okay, maybe this will work out. But do you have any idea how lucky you are? It was just by sheer coincidence I was in the 911 dispatch room when the call came in. It's a good thing I live close to here. I stepped in and told the dispatch crew I would personally respond to the call."

"Tell me about that call—who made it?"

"Someone here on the staff, I guess. I don't know—it's not important."

"It is to me. I want to hear that call."

"That can be arranged—give me some time."

"No—I want to hear it now."

"Man, it's not safe. I can't bring you into the station to listen right after me personally handling the call. It will draw suspicion."

"Playing it safe? I told you—that is not the way to re-assert our power."

"What's so damn important about who called? One of the staff caught wind of your antics and blew the whistle."

"No way! Since I got out, I've worked hard to get them in my pocket—paid them off too many times. I want to know—prove to myself—it's him."

"Him? Him who?"

"That meddling little gargoyle. Remember the Tard? He's still around—been fucking up my life for years."

* * *

KNEW IT—FELT IT. I WISHED—PRAYED that Matt would save me. It was difficult to concentrate on my good thoughts. To not really know what they do to me, I sort of black out.

There was a commotion—shouts and shuffling. The woman left—fast. I hope they never come back.

I hate to agree with Rat Rattigan on anything, but I'm certain that Matt is involved with the 911 call.

* * *

THE CONVERSATION – PART THREE

MATT BROKE THE SILENCE. "MAYBE another drink *is* in order."

Jude said nothing. A stunned expression covered his face.

"I'll take your silence as a 'yes'."

Matt poured. Jude did not keep with his pledge. Matt resumed telling his story.

"My mother's mental state was fragile. Of course, your father knew that."

Jude downed his drink in one gulp. "Is this why you know so much about my father?"

"We'll get to that."

"I feel I may regret this. Go on."

"Blackman, Rattigan, and Landis always handled private matters for our family. Your father…until his suicide…" Matt waited for Jude's remark of protest. None came.

"…your father…he handled the probate of the estate. Other than the mansion there wasn't much left—just enough to run the household for a while. The size of the place and its operating costs proved to be too much, and it had to be sold. The need to sell and my mother's mental state meant your father was around…too often."

Jude finally showed signs of life. "What do you mean by that?"

"Add two and two."

"You can't mean…"

"There you go again."

"What?"

"Playing naïve."

"C'mon. I…"

"…know better…and you know what kind of man your father was."

"I'm just a reporter."

"A reporter who knows people should have done something."

"Look—I was just a kid when all that happened. I wasn't involved and, anyway, it was long ago."

"From naive to not involved. For you it's just so much ancient history."

"It's over."

"Things like this are never over."

"What do you mean?"

"Effects, repercussions, loose strings."

"Which have nothing to do with me."

"Really?"

"What are you driving at?"

"You are still acting naïve."

"Maybe I'm just stupid, but how can any of this really have anything to do with me?"

"Oh, brother, does it ever."

"I don't see how."

"Well, brother…"

"Stop it."

"Stop what?"

"Stop calling me brother."

"Why? You really are my *brother*."

This time, the silence was truly deafening.

SOMETHING WICKED
THIS WAY COMES

LASER BEAMS SHOT FROM MYA'S magnificent green eyes. "Matt, don't even think about stalling on giving me an answer," she said, crossing her arms. "Something is up, and I want to know what it is."

"I can't imagine what you are talking about."

"I told you—no stalling—out with it." Her interruption was quick and hard.

"Ah, Mya…" Matt squirmed and batted his eyes.

"No! Cut the act—you're hiding something."

Matt ignored her remark. "Rattigan is out—and here again."

"Watching. I knew it—felt it."

"Yes, but he's been passive."

"I don't believe you."

"For real…"

"Read my lips. I…do…not…believe…you."

"Okay—okay. I'll explain." He paused.

"So? I'm waiting."

"He's hassling with Richard."

"Hassling? What do you mean by that?"

"You know… He's been…been…"

"Been what?"

"I've reason to more than just suspect Rat is using him in a terrible scam. And if rumors are true, it's got a kinky sex component in it."

"Oh my God—that sick pervert."

"I think if I get enough to nail him, he'll be gone for good."

"But how has he been able to get away with what you suspect he is doing?"

"I don't know. He's been lucky—and I've been unlucky. One of the few decent staff members still working at the home tipped me off, but it was my bad luck that the nine-one-one call was answered by one of Rattigan's pals."

"Is there anything more you can do?"

"I'm trying. Through others I've attempted to have Richard moved to another facility, but the state has always maintained that Richard is its ward. Bureaucracy being what it is means he's stuck in the lowest-cost dump they could find. And then there is the problem with me. I have zero credibility as me. I have a plan, but the reliability of my potential helper is uncertain."

"Matt, maybe you need to re-evaluate your position regarding Richard. He's been unresponsive for years. Is protecting a comatose body truly that important?"

"He's not unresponsive—that's why he's abused. *Think about it.* Anything can be done to a sleeping victim. Imagine sexual perversion and—."

"Stop—it's too gross. I can't think of it." Mya was shaken.

She turned to another line of thought to flee what she imagined. *From the day I first saw him, I wanted him always to be part of my life. He has a presence that is beyond all others. I wish I could capture what he is and share it with the world.*

The fear of *No Matt* prompted her to prompt him. "Matt, I haven't forgotten."

"Forgotten what?"

"About you stalling. Remember?"

"Oh—that."

"Yes—that. Rattigan could be coming after you. He will figure out it was you who called nine-one-one—or he'll just blame you anyway. Is that what has you acting weird?"

"Not entirely."

"Then what is it? You know me—I'll pester you until I get the truth."

"Don't pester me. Just don't."

"Then out with it."

"Okay—but let me do it my way."

"What other way is there?"

"Look—Mick…I…I…"

She knew he was avoiding something serious. Matt only called her Mick when he had something extremely important to share, or worse when he was hiding something. She knew him well enough.

He'll shift gears as a diversion, she correctly thought. *And here it comes.*

"Dietrologia. What do you know about it?"

"Another ploy to derail me?"

"No—no! There are more people like Rattigan than you can imagine. Dietrologia is about that—really—it's the science of what is behind something. Dark things. It's not conspiracy stuff—it is seriously about The Darkness."

"Yeah—dark baloney."

"Please—follow me on this. There is a big Darkness—and the smaller stuff is part and parcel of it. Everything is derivative—like when a particular thing inspires another thing. Take ideas, in books there may be an idea that influences—inspires—creates another. One writer pens an idea through a term or phrase which advances another idea in the mind of another writer, on and on it goes. It's the same with music, sculpture—even dance. Now, imagine the whole thing is connected, orchestrated, by a being or force. Something that is behind it all. The effort to find that something is dietrologia."

"Good try. Another one of your Matt Facts? Just another ploy to put me off track. I think you're afraid I'll ask, 'Does this have anything to do with Claudia?'"

"Okay, okay—I guess you win."

"Ha! You never guess at anything. Now I know why you are stalling. It's your health—right?"

He tried to avoid the issue. "Give me some time to think how best to—"

She interrupted him. "Stop playing around. Quit stalling me."

"Really, I'm not."

"Well?" She crossed her arms and pouted. "How long are you going to take?"

"Alright, but don't overreact…I'm thinking about going away."

"Going away?"

"Leaving Lancaster."

"You can't."

"I can't?"

"I mean—you've never been more than a couple dozen miles away from here."

"That should be enough reason for me to leave, don't you think? Maybe it's time for me to actually see the world and experience life outside of this one spot on the map."

"But—you've always made it a point *not* to leave. Why the decision? And why now?"

"It's time."

"Time for *what*?"

"Time for a change."

"You sound like a cheap politician."

"Are you trying to be funny?"

"All I know is you're acting strange, and you leaving is not the kind of change I want. In fact, I don't want anything to change—not now. The shop is finally turning a profit, I'm painting enough to see an actual show for my paintings in the near future, we visit and—"

He interrupted, "Mick."

"What?"

"I *have* to go."

"Why do you *have* to go? Where?"

"It just means my time here is almost up."

"That's ridiculous. Almost up—from what? That is beyond ridiculous."

"Not from my point of view."

"Which makes absolutely no sense."

"Making sense or not—I'm still leaving. But before I do, I've got to eradicate a threat and make arrangements for Richard."

"I *still* don't like it."

"Please, Mick—I'm ready for this."

"What is 'this'?"

"The change—my change. It's my time. Things have to change."

"I told you I don't want anything to change."

"You just said I should re-think Richard—that's change."

"That's different."

"How?"

"I don't know—it just is."

"That makes no sense."

She sent him another one of her green-eyed laser shots. "I just...just don't want you to go. You are the best friend I have."

Matt scrunched his face sideways, and in his finest Stallone impression quipped, "Sometimes a man's gotta do what a man's gotta do."

"Don't do that. Hiding in humor is just another deception."

"Mick—look at me. Really take a long look. Making jokes, hiding—what else do I have?"

Mya's response was to give him a hug. Matt hugged back and felt her unattainability in his arms—the longing that could never be fulfilled.

She felt his disappointment, the ache, and the pain. Mya disengaged, painted her face with a smile and forced a weak laugh out into the infinite vacuum between them. She ached, too. The unattainable in her fled. She smiled, this time for real.

Matt smiled, too, as his ailing sorrow-filled heart yearned, *Maybe, just maybe. Maybe.* He silently prayed. *Oh God, I could live with just a maybe.*

The taste of his desperation filled the air, and he croaked, "I think I should go."

And he did.

* * *

HIS LONELINESS IS PALPABLE. EVEN the times they have the happiest of visits, Matt is always sad at the end. Their times together are all alike—ends.

One night, Matt read to me this story. No hiding, no deception. Just a lot of love. It's his longing, for a beautiful love story—the one he will never have.

* * *

THE RED DRESS

by Otto Janus

WHO HE?

"Calvin O'Donnell?" I blurted out. "He's a nobody. Why should I waste time on him?"

My statement was a reflex, an over-heated reaction to being given an unwanted assignment. Jim, my partner, was leaving town for a week and I would have to work alone. The volume and tone of my voice had nothing to do with O'Donnell. For me, he was merely one of those plodding, get-along-go-along, average sort of guys I could barely recall from somewhere in the past.

To tell the truth, if a thug put a gun to my head demanding, "Tell me something about O'Donnell, or else." I would have to remain silent and become a crime statistic. For the life of me I could not remember anything about the man. O'Donnell was nothing to me. I was mad for a different reason.

When Jim dropped into his goodbye remarks that along with everything else dumped on me, I was to pen O'Donnell's obit as the lead feature for the weekend edition of our small-town newspaper—I blew a fuse. I didn't like that he was getting away for an entire week leaving me to do e-v-e-r-y-t-h-i-n-g.

"The funeral is the day after tomorrow," Jim informed me. "But there will be multiple viewings... to accommodate the crowds. You'll have plenty of time to get some good stuff for an in-depth story."

I complained again. "He's a nobody."

Jim pushed back, "You're wrong. Everyone who is anybody around Woodstown knows Calvin O'Donnell."

"Well, I don't," I shot back. I instantly regretted my reply.

Jim gave me that look. The one he had shared on several occasions since I had returned home with my tail between my legs. Jim and I were the same age. We grew up together—joined at the hip until we graduated high school. When a situation called for "the big-brother tone" to be used, Jim used it. Without skipping a beat he preached like an older sibling.

"Like I said…folks from around here know him." Jim pointed toward the paper's records room, which also served as my makeshift office, and finished with, "You might take a peek in there."

I threw my hands up, turned, and retreated steeped in defeat. "Okay—okay. I know what this means…"

From behind, his big brother voice sliced me in two. "You knew this day would come. I'm going on vacation. It's time to step outside and face life again."

In the blink of an eye, life—or at least the main parts of it—can leap through your brain. Everything that matters is clear to see. Jim was the catalyst for such an event.

I stopped, turned, and stared at my life-long friend. Decades peeled away, but we were standing in the same office. As kids, we worked there part-time for my father who owned the paper back then. I did so reluctantly and with an ample amount of seething belligerence. Jim was totally opposite to me. He loved everything about the paper. I hated *The Gazette* and all it stood for. The *Woodstown Rag* was what I called it.

Like I said, Jim loved the paper—also my dad and the community they served. In our late teens our opposing views worked themselves out.

We went our separate ways. Jim never left Woodstown, or the paper. He kept working for my dad and I made my escape from Salem County, New Jersey. While Jim patched a degree together with night classes at a string of colleges within driving distance of his news beat, I raced across the border to Penn State on a mixed sports and academic ride.

After playing ball, I coasted through law school, headed to a prime Philly firm, and vowed I would never come back to small town life. But, two decades and a bit later I slithered into Woodstown and hid in the backroom, making believe that my job as Associate Editor was real.

In fact, my title was as phony as my lame-ass return to Woodstown. The safety-net position I had was Jim's way to thank my father for selling him the paper instead of including it in his estate. Dad knew I'd dump *The Gazette* if I ever got control of it. He sold it to Jim knowing that Jim would carry on the work I had always denied as being important. When the sale took place, I did not care. Only later did it affect me—when I needed a place to land.

I made a mess of life. Divorced, remarried, divorced again, facing bankruptcy and living inside a bottle—that is how I stumbled through two decades in the big city.

I capped off my tenure at the firm by screwing up the estate plan of one of Philadelphia's most

beloved public figures. Fortunately, the firm's mal-
practice insurance covered my mistake and there
was no scandal. I narrowly avoided disbarment and
its public embarrassment by agreeing to disappear
and never practice law again. That is how and why I
returned to Woodstown. Jim gave me a place to lick
my wounds, and today he was kicking me out into
the world to test how I have healed.

Jim followed me into my hiding place. "Meet
me at Paulson's Funeral Home in an hour. I want to
be at the head of the line to pay my respects. It's on
my way out of town—I'll get you started," he said
in an assuring tone.

I grabbed a fresh reporter's notepad and said,
"No. I'm good." Eyeballing him with as much resolve
as I could muster, I said, "I wasn't trying to skate out
on anything—really. I knew this time would come."

Jim eyed me back. "You sure you are okay with
this?"

"Yep," I told him. "You never miss The Masters.
Get over to Paulson's, make your appearance, leave
town, and go eat pimento cheese sandwiches until
the azaleas wilt. I'm okay. I'll be right behind you."
I punctuated my bravado with a big smile.

I passed test number one. Jim was convinced I
was ready to fly solo again. He pointed at my computer. "Skip our records. Cal O'Donnell wasn't a

* * *

You Never Know What
You Don't Know

JIM WAS RIGHT. THERE WAS next to nothing in our little community newspaper's records—just a birth notice from the same week as mine.

Mumbling to myself, I asked, "Why am I wasting time on this guy?"

Calvin O'Donnell was definitely not a star—not even a memorable also-ran.

I looked at the corner of my office. It was filled with a jumbled pile of boxes. My personal effects had been pared down by my divorces and the nearly avoided scandal. The pile was not much of a legacy.

"Yay!" I congratulated myself, as I reached into one of the boxes to extract my high school yearbook. "I can't remember him, but he's sure to be in here."

Moments later I was staring at the Cal O'Donnell of thirty years ago. At first glance, O'Donnell looked like the sort of guy who would probably have been invisible to me back then. But, looking back at me was an exceptional set of eyes housed in his average frame. I guess I never got close enough to see the character pouring out through his gaze upon the world. I just never saw it.

The caption under the picture read: *A friend to all, Cal aspires to be the flow instead of just going with it.*

Normally the quips and quotes that summed up a student were meant to sit above the list of clubs, activities, teams, and awards, which defined a person's high school experience. For Calvin O'Donnell there was nothing beyond that brief descriptive statement.

"Nothing?" I remarked with faked hurt. I tossed the book into the pile and scolded the collective mess that was my past, "Thanks. I guess this means I really do go old school on this assignment."

I jammed the notepad into my pocket and headed to my car.

The drive to Paulson's took all of three minutes. I should have walked. The parking lot was full, as were all the adjacent streets. I found a spot several blocks away and pondered the situation. Jim wasn't kidding—it looked like half the county was there. I saw Jim and waved. He gave me a thumbs up to let me know he knew I was "on the job." I passed the final test. The paper was my responsibility for a week.

Paulson's inside was more crowded than out on the street. There was a crowd waiting to sign in at the table where a remembrance/memorial book would normally be placed. Today there were two books. For a guy not in the paper's files he was extremely popular.

From behind, my elbow was grabbed and heard a voice loudly exclaim, "I can't believe it. The rumor was spread you had returned. It's really you." Meg Reece, local diva, world-class bitch, and my one-time girlfriend was the source of the loud comment.

Wanting to maintain the decorum expected at Paulson's, I whispered, "Hello, Meg."

She ignored my cue, and boomed, "Woodstown is a small town. I was certain I'd see you, but nnnooooo. Jim has been hiding you like Anne Frank." She snort-laughed and went on, "Catching up with you at a funeral home—can you imagine that?" Again, her voice was louder than required and about half of the mourners waiting near the table stared at us.

A clammy sweat popped out of my every pore. "A coming-out party was not on my agenda today, Meg." I pulled out my notebook. "I'm sorry, but I can't talk to you right now—got work to do." I made eye contact with the closest stranger near the table and approached him, leaving a bug-eyed Meg behind.

That was it. Out of my hiding place, on the job, no Jim to protect me—I was a reporter, not the gnome of the records room.

"Excuse me," I addressed my target, a swarthy middle-aged man of mid years. "I'm with the *Gazette.* Would you be willing to share something about Calvin O'Donnell?"

"Sure," my first interviewee said. "What do you want to know?"

"Just tell me who you are and how you are connected to Mr. O'Donnell."

"I'm Ben Vitto. Cal was my friend. But that's no big deal." He motioned to the crowded room and smiled. "I'd say everyone here is a friend of his."

"Yeah, it's quite a turnout. I stalled trying to think of what to ask next. Yes, I was reporter, but I was an inexperienced one. Vitto sensed my lack of direction and went on without me.

"I guess what you want to know is what it is about Cal that brings me and all these people here. Right?"

I nodded as I looked about. The place was not only packed—it was filled with the most diverse crowd I could ever imagine being assembled in Woodstown. There were all the usual types one might expect to see, but also many unexpected additions peppered in as singles, pairs, and small groups. I recognized western-dressed performers and hands from the Cowtown Rodeo, priests, Orthodox and Roman Catholic, more clergy, artsy types, working-class men and women, and suits of all types. Jim was right, everyone knew this guy.

"Yes—yes," I said. "That's exactly what I want. What made him so special?"

"Well…Cal had an ability to sense when people were in need of help. And he was *always* willing to do something about it. He *never* sat on the sidelines—he acted."

"Is that how it was for you? How did you meet him?"

"I'm from over in Buena—Italian-American through-and-through. My family has been farming there forever. But contracting is my line of business—homes, small commercial buildings, and some government stuff. Do you know Buena?"

"Yeah—was raised in Woodstown."

"Then you know about the Shrine…"

"No."

"The Padre Pio Shrine. Where have you been?

"I….ah…."

"Never mind," he said, paying me no mind. "I built it. Did the construction and all."

"And Cal O'Donnell helped, right?" It was a weak recovery, but a recovery nonetheless.

Ben continued. "No—Cal didn't help with the building. He came in later—when it was dedicated. He saved the day."

It was then that I remembered my notepad in my hand and nodded for Vitto to go on.

"Cal was working on another one of my jobs. He was a jack-of-all trades and I had him troubleshooting a pesky electrical re-do on a commercial site. If you ever had a problem—of any type—you called him. Did I tell you he was a jack-of-all trades?"

"Yes," I answered as I hid an eye roll.

Vitto went on. "I guess he overheard my bitching about the tie-in box with New Jersey Electric. I was afraid the system, as designed, wouldn't take the massive short-term load the dedication would place on it. You know—lights, news trucks—all the one-time extras. We blew out some of the lights when we tested 'em."

I faked knowing all about electrical mysteries, and said "Yeah, yeah," as I kept nodding.

He continued. "I was at the shrine and getting nowhere with the doofus sent out by Jersey Electric—and guess who shows up?"

"Cal."

"Right!" Vitto beamed. "Cal's got a load of temp lights and a generator in his pickup. We tie his rig into the system and boom! We got power out the ying-yang and at the dedication everything went smooth as silk. Cal just knew what was needed and was there, Johnny-on-the-Spot like. He's been a friend ever since. And although he never was a church goer just look over there." He pointed to the priests who were in the midst of what looked like a church gathering. "That group is chock-full of ministers, street preachers, and the like. In one way or another, Cal O'Donnell helped them all."

I thanked him and moved on. Going from group to group, in short order I had dozens of versions of the same story. Every account centered upon a stranger, or casual acquaintance, facing a challenge and becoming a friend through Cal O'Donnell's thoughtful, kind, and timely actions. It was if he had some form of ESP which brought him opportunities to display his unique problem-solving abilities.

O'Donnell's efforts were not limited to charitable acts. Ross Campbell, the owner of the Oak Road Vineyard, recounted how Cal worked day and night "like it was his own place and money at stake" to prepare the vineyard for its very first pressing. "We are what we are today because he cared so much," Campbell shared with a sincere and open affection that at one time I would have derided as "small town schmaltz" but now saw as being real and admirable.

It made no difference. Whether it was clergy, homemakers, professionals, or blue-collar laborers, all who were assembled spoke highly and with affection about the man lying at rest in the next room.

* * *

A Step into the Past

I KNEW IT WOULD HAVE DONE no good to remind Jim I am not one to attend wakes and funerals. Just peeking into the viewing room from the entry hall took a lot of determination, but I was keenly interested in Calvin O'Donnell. I had to see him. With trepidation, I entered the room and stood in the viewing line.

The line moved slowly. The people ahead of me were mourners wishing to say goodbye to the man I had earlier called a nobody. I thought about all the comments I had heard and unsuccessfully combed through my memory. Woodstown was so small and I could not recall meeting or knowing Calvin O'Donnell during my formative years. I had been totally blind to his existence.

When it came to be my turn to approach the coffin, I froze for a few moments. Other than for my father I had religiously avoided such situations. Thankfully, no one noticed my anxiety or the delay.

The man at rest looked like an older sleeping version of the photo in the high school annual. Without those mesmerizing eyes, he was very average. I paid my respects in the minimum amount of time and moved away. My next move was to address the O'Donnell family.

Through my interviews I had learned that Calvin O'Donnell's immediate family consisted of a loving wife and four children. As I approached them to express sympathy, I saw three twenty-somethings and a teenager seated near a woman with her back toward me.

"Mrs. O'Donnell." I said softly.

The woman, in possession of a subtle natural beauty, looked toward me. "Yes," she responded, showing the slightest amount of recognition. "Jim said you would be coming."

Her response, coupled with the unusual situation, confounded me and again I froze. "I—I—I…" My brain could not instruct my mouth on what to say.

She smiled, reached for my hand, and brought me into her circle. "Please sit with us for a while."

Feeling the request was also part instruction, I took a seat and stared at this peculiarly familiar stranger. Her green eyes sparkled and a moment from my past exploded in my memory. "Jennie?" I asked. "Jennie Pollard?"

"Yes—you remember," she said.

"Emily's friend. When my cousin Emily came to visit, you played with her."

"Yes, her coming to visit was special. How is she?"

"Okay...I guess. I don't really know." I was embarrassed by my answer and Jennie sensed it. She quickly changed the subject, bringing it back to the reason I was there.

"Jim told me you would be writing something about Cal."

I was grateful for her cue. I motioned toward the line and the crowd still waiting,

"I had no idea how well known he is—I—ah—ah. I mean was—I mean... I don't even remember him." The awkwardness of my statement hit me. I shut up.

Jennie spoke after what seemed an eternity. She nodded toward the growing line wishing to address her and her children. "Perhaps tomorrow morning would be a good time for me to share what I can to help you with your assignment. Would that be all right?"

"Yes," I answered. "I'd like that."

She told me where to be. I moved away to be quickly replaced by one of the many mourners who came to pay their respects to the man I wished to know about.

* * *

A NEW DAY

The O'Donnell property was on the edge of town and was easy to find. When I got there, I found a short driveway skirting a commercial building signed as O'DONNELL'S MACHINING, FABRICATION, ELECTRICAL, AND REPAIR. A private roadway led me to a neatly trimmed yard before an ample rancher surrounded by parked cars. It appeared the Paulson crowd had merely moved its location. I parked and joined the stream of people going in and out of the residence.

Inside, I found the aura was markedly different than the night before. People talked loudly as they milled about. Without the presence a coffin there was no muting of expression. It was near chaos, but positive—an event, definitely not a wake. It was a respectful and joyous family-like celebration of the life of a departed head of the clan.

Jennie seemingly stepped out of nowhere. "It's always been like this," she said. She looked tired, lessened by the crowd. I sensed she needed to talk. "Cal was a magnet," she explained. "A positive magnet." Her green eyes pierced me. "I want people to know that about him."

She directed me into a small room, one I believe used by her for crafts, hobbies, and the like. To start my interview, I began with my ignorance. "How did I not know Cal, or at least know of him when I lived here?" I asked.

Jennie smiled. "You didn't have the time. You were the hero back then—remember?"

"Me—a hero?"

"Oh, yes. You starred in football, excelled at school—catapulted out of here and gave those of us behind an example on how to escape. On the other hand, Cal was plain and simple. He worked with his hands—a trait, or skill, that had grown out of favor. Plus, in those days, he avoided sticking out. He did not like being seen."

"I'm amazed." I gestured at the throng outside the room and asked, "What happened to cause all that?"

"It was cumulative. Cal was a good person who just kept being good. He was focused and methodical in his goodness and what you see is the result—a life that touched so many other lives."

"Amazing," I mumbled, "It's just amazing."

"Yes. And that's what I want you to write about—how amazing he was because he was so consistently good."

"And you watched it all? From the beginning to…to…"

I found it impossible to complete the sentence. She finished for me.

"The end. You can say it." She waited a moment, then added, "And I'm fine dealing with him being gone."

"Really?"

"Yes. The diagnosis was a shock at first, but its seriousness prepared me for his leaving. Pancreatic cancer is quick."

I groped my mind to find a method to go on, but nothing was there.

She finally said, "Remember, I said those of us left behind looked to you as an example."

"Me? An example?"

"As the way out of here—to escape small-town America."

"I'm back. I guess, whatever it was, it didn't work. What about you? You're here, too."

She sighed and waited a moment. Then she said, "Oh, I left all right…your example inspired me."

"*That* I have to hear about."

"I was three years behind you in school. We all knew about your success—playing Penn State football and at the same time being a scholar in their English department—hometown pride and all that."

"I guess I had no idea about things back here."

"Why would you? Life here was to be escaped, which you did. I did, too. Made it all the way to New York, by way of Columbia's theater arts program."

"Wow—Columbia is one of the best. What happened?"

"Maybe it was just too much, too soon. Big city burnout is what I call it…" She trailed off and gazed out the window. I respected her need to have a patch of privacy and waited. After a few moments she continued.

"I worked my way from the classroom to some off-Broadway and experimental productions—none of them memorable. The artsy life ate me up. The end came when I landed in the ER. I was drunk, doped, and spent like a used prop. Cal heard about it from his sister—Meg had been my life-long friend. I had no clue as to how he felt about me, but I soon learned. It was Cal who came to New York and brought me home. Up 'til then I had no idea he cared specifically about me. He was just good to everyone. I never thought his attention to me was special."

"When did things change—I mean between you and Cal?"

"A couple weeks after he brought me home Cal made it plain how he felt. He told me how he wanted me to remain here—with him. But he wanted me to figure out where I wanted to be. I had always dreamed of being gone from here, but New York changed all that. It was very apparent to me some dreams can become nightmares and I stayed."

"No regrets?"

"None. Cal made certain of that."

"How so? What do you mean?"

"Through Meg he had a window into my world—my dream world. I did not realize until later—when Cal and I were together—how many times I had shared with Meg my dream of performing on Broadway as *The Lady in Red*. She shared with him how that dream senselessly motivated me to be in the theater. He figured it all out and found a way of dealing with that illusion."

I know I must have looked very perplexed. Jennie chuckled. It was the first non-mourning expression I had seen on her. She got up and stood by the window, looking out. Her voice sounded as if she was somewhere back in time.

"Cal was not only good—he was funny." She laughed., "One day, early in his courting process, he arrived with a package. He was acting all secret-like and serious, but he was smiling and joking, too. It drove me nuts. I was being pampered by everyone— Mom, Dad, Meg, everybody who knew me—they all walked around on eggshells, not wanting to bring up my failed attempt at fame and fortune. But Cal, he would not go their way. He attacked straight on. That day Cal gave me the package and proposed at the same time. 'Here,' he said, 'whenever you get the urge—put it on and we'll party up a storm.'"

"What was in the package?"

"A red dress—a beautiful red dress."

"So, you could be *The Lady in Red*."

"Exactly—and I was—Oh, I was," she said, with a tinge in her voice that told me the dress was so much more than an article of clothing.

"Right then, I said, 'Yes.' It was on a Saturday. We went out and had a wonderful time. And every time thereafter—it was always on a Saturday I put on my red dress for Cal and lived my dream."

The male in me balked at saying, "It sounds so… so…."

"Romantic. No way around it. Cal was a good man and devising romantic escapes was his other talent."

I could say nothing. I sat there in awe of what I was experiencing. Since returning to Woodstown I had hid, floundered, hid some more, and avoided exactly the type of life being revealed to me. I wanted to hear more—all of it.

Nights in Red

I LET JENNIE TALK. IT WAS good therapy—for the both of us. She was letting go of an important part of her life and I was grasping to find something to make mine livable again.

"That first night we went to a movie, for a walk, and then to the Dairy Dip. It was the beginning of a tradition for us. For almost three decades, at least once a month—sometimes more, sometimes less—I'd put on my red dress and the two of us stepped into our own private world."

She walked to the closet, opened the door, and reached in. Her hand came out holding a red dress of dated style. Jennie beamed when she shared, "I have celebrated, partied, danced, and cried in this dress. It has been mended so many times I can't count the number."

Even from a distance it was apparent the dress had seen a good deal of use.

"That first night a little boy's ice cream cone dribbled on me. I got very upset. But Cal, as only he could, made it into something special by pledging to love me in this dress no matter how worn, torn, or stained it became."

She touched the dress with care and explained. "When we were first married, money was tight, so we often stayed at home. Later, when we could afford more in life, I refused to replace it. Heavens—it's even been re-dyed."

"Re-dyed—can you do that?"

"Yes. Our eldest daughter, Lynne grabbed it out of the closet one September and used it on one of the Halloween displays along Main Street. Neither Cal nor I had the heart to tell her she had taken something special—so the red dress was on display outside for close to a month and faded to a sort of red with pink highlights." She laughed. "It really got a major overhaul that year."

"Obviously, it has become quite an heirloom."

"Yes—it's a piece of history now." She gently placed it back in the closet and continued, "Cal liked to joke about my dress being the best investment he ever made." She sighed, "He was so right—he was right about so many things."

"From all I've learned so far, he had amazing insight and judgment."

"Yes. And that is what I want you to write about—just Cal, not us, not me, and not the dress. I think it would be good if you stayed here today talking to his friends—and then do the same again this evening at the second viewing. Would you do that?"

Of course I said, "Yes."

"That's good," she said. "Jim has been protecting you for a long time. A tribute to Cal will be a prefect way for you to re-join the community."

I looked at her with puzzlement. "I don't understand—I—"

"It's been decades, but those of us who knew you then still know you now. You always had the talent to write…so write. Write about Cal. And promise you will not include anything about me, or the dress. Just write about Cal."

* * *

SUCCESS IS SPELLED L-O-V-E

AND WRITE I DID. BUT only after I listened to everything I could about Cal O'Donnell.

I remained that day at his home, absorbed more of who and what he was, and that night I attended the second viewing.

Later, I participated in an impromptu Irish-drunken wake with his closest friends. The funeral ceremony and burial ended my research and information gathering. I followed Jennie's direction—with a passion.

The result was a lengthy obituary that covered more space than any article ever did in the history of the paper.

Jim was dumbfounded upon reading it when he returned. "I never expected this," he said quietly as he put his copy down. "I don't know what to say. I told you to write his obit. You penned a biography."

"I know it's a bit long," I countered defensively.

He stared at the title, THE VALUE OF ONE LIFE. "An obit with a headline?"

"Artistic license," I quipped, ready for an argument, but got none.

"What's the reaction been?"

"Excellent! Every copy has been sold," I said with pride. "The extra sales more than cover the costs."

"I meant the family—how have they responded?"

"Can't say."

"Huh?" To this bit of news, he showed dismay.

To defend myself I quickly said, "I've called the home number several times and have only been able to leave voice messages. There have been no calls back and out of respect to Jennie and the children, I thought it would be a bit too self-serving to drop in unexpected just to ask, 'How'd you like the obit?' I'll keep trying—"

"No, no need to—it's a small town. You'll hear from the family when it's time. Things will sort themselves out."

I followed his lead, based upon the fact Jim had successfully lived in Woodstown while I had squandered my life away. And that's how I played it.

Papers in Philly, Wilmington, Baltimore, and multiple points in-between ran summaries and commentaries on my treatment of Cal's life and death. Some even ran the entire piece. The unprecedented attention paid my writing soon created momentum sufficient to relocate me from my hiding place into the paper's main office. It was there I assumed the actual duties associated with my title.

In short, I started anew.

I recognize I owe much in my current life to Calvin O'Donnell's death, and I am ashamed to admit that a portion of my self-absorbing nature survived. I never closed the loop with Jennie and her children.

But I did keep track of them, or at least Jennie. And I believe that is why I did not close the loop. As I waxed normal, Jennie waned. As Jim constantly reminds me…Woodstown is a small town. The local buzz was Jennie was not handling her loss very well. No one—and I mean no one—could reverse her steady decline. And it was no surprise when the same verbal telegraph spread the news Jennie had died of what could only be described as a broken heart.

There was no need for Jim to assign the story. Guilt is a great motivator. I was in touch with Cal Junior almost immediately.

"She was avoiding everyone," he said. "She wasn't avoiding you."

"But I should have been more persistent," I responded. "I'm sorry that—"

He stopped me. "No apology is needed."

It was one of those awkward moments of closeness between people who have a single strong link to bind them and nothing else beyond. I looked at this carbon copy of Cal and could only offer a nod and dumb smile. It was so little, but I wanted it to project so much.

Junior nodded back and softly said, "Mom—and all of us in the family—liked your story about Dad very much." His look was sincere. I was relieved.

He reached into his pocket and produced an envelope. "Here—Mom told me to give this to you."

Cal Junior shook my hand and departed, leaving me with a note with a brief message: THANK YOU FOR WRITING SO WELL ABOUT MY CAL. I RELEASE YOU FROM YOUR PROMISE ABOUT MY DRESS. It was simply signed, *Jennie.*

Again, I attended the viewings and visited the home. The funeral is today and I will of course sit through the service and ride in the long motorcade to the cemetery.

So…what have I learned?

Woodstown is a small town and it has taught me something important—something *I know.* It is not a belief. It is truth.

Love is real.

They say love is everywhere, but we just fail to see it. I know love is real because I saw it today—real love. It radiated from Jennie O'Donnell lying in state at Paulson's Funeral Home. She was at peace… smiling…wearing a well-worn red dress.

* * *

I N HIS HEART MATT IS a pure romantic. It is the cross he struggles to carry every day. He knows there is no hope for *The Red Dress* sort of story in his life, but he believes in its beauty and writes about it for others to contemplate.

Whenever I think about the Mya-Matt thing I am drawn to an anthology of poems Matt published under his pen name. As with books of poems, sales were very modest. Established writers are granted the luxury seeing their verse in print based upon the popularity of their other work. This very brief poem is the one I remember.

Haunted in the loneliness of lust / wanting to be with more than self / wanting to be touched / joined / dreaming of her caress. / Driven by the loneliness of lust / one wants, needs touch / to recognize, value, and desire more than soul.

* * *

NEARER TO THE ALTAR

ARE YOU STILL HERE? I think everything is buzzing around me again. It's like that day in the alley. The dark is hovering. I wish I could travel to the future and know. I want to visit Father Alexios. Maybe I'll find him praying.

He prays a lot. In fact, he prays more than anyone I have ever encountered when I fly. I know he believes his prayers are heard. I'm not convinced, but I have an open mind about the entire practice.

At times it seems prayers are answered.

What I do find peculiar is the modern world, filled with all sorts of WI-FI devices, is full of people who mock prayer.

But prayers are visible just as much as WI-FI signals—which is not at all. The mockers ought to ponder that there could be something to it. After all, there is an app for prayer.

* * *

FATHER PAUL FROWNED AND THOUGHT, *No doubt about it, something is about to happen; a note from Matthias, a call from, Claudia, his doctor, and a nagging feeling something is amiss. This is not a routine day. I am worried.*

Speaking to Matt's note, he asked, "What is this all about?"

* * *

WHEN MATT ARRIVED, HE WAS not his usual plucky self. He appeared distracted, even distraught.

"What in heaven's name has happened to you?"

"Not me, Father. It's my friend, Richard—he's being abused."

"Tell me everything."

Matt explained what he suspected was occurring in the Parker Home and how several staff members reached out to him and shared their suspicions. Father Paul knew how the privileged members of the community closed ranks to protect their offspring years ago, but he was not prepared for what Matthias described.

"If what you think is true, I'm infuriated. We have a serious problem to address."

"I have a plan, but it needs you in it, at the end, particularly if anything goes wrong." The priest leaned in for details of his role. "Father, I need you to shepherd Richard's move away from the Parker Home. Your credibility in the community, and some resources I can get to you will be crucial in protecting him."

"Of course, whatever is needed I am with you—and I mean *whatever*."

"Thank you—I am getting the resources and a team together. Which means I need to get moving." Matt started for the door.

"Not so fast, Matthias. We need to talk—about *another* pressing matter."

Matt halted. "I know that tone and inflection. Unspoken communication at its best. What's up?"

"I had a call…"

"And?"

"It was Claudia."

"About?"

Father Paul gave his best *don't-play-with-me* look. "Let's—you and me—talk about your health instead of our usual theology-oriented topics. Okay?"

"Okay."

"As they say, 'it's your turn.' Start right after the 'it's no big deal' full-of-bull mantra where you always hide within when it comes to discussing your health."

Matt squirmed. "You got me." He paused. Then Matt confessed, "It's bad."

"How bad?"

"Bad enough for, 'I am an image of your ineffable glory. Lead me back to your likeness and renew me. Grant me the homeland for which I long.'"

Matt turned and left. No look back. No goodbye.

Father Paul was struck mute. He immediately recognized Matt's recital of portions of the Orthodox Memorial Service.

Once recovered, he made his way to the church's sanctuary to pray for his friend's health and well-being.

* * *

I FEEL A SECOND DARKNESS LOOMING. My selfish response is based in my need for Matt as a friend. I don't know what will happen to me in a world without him. It scares me.

And I worry about a world without his light in it.

＊ ＊ ＊

A Plan

JUDE'S MIND IS WHIRLING ABOUT, in an effort to find its center point. *Concentrate. Concentrate. Concentrate.* My mantra is ineffective. *Concentrate. Concentrate. Concentrate.* He stares into space. *Concentrate. Concentrate. Concentrate.* Doodling is an effort. *Concentrate. Concentrate. Concentrate.*

"I give up," he mutters, finding himself reading the placard taped to the Joey Votto bobble-head sitting on Yvonne's desk. The placard reads: I LOVE MY COMPUTER; ALL MY FRIENDS ARE IN IT.

"Stars and celebrities can say almost anything," Jude says to Yvonne. She pops her head up from the depths of her confines.

"What do you mean?"

Jude asks, "What color is three p.m.?"

Counter question. "Are you feeling alright?"

"How much does green weigh?" Jude is on a roll. "What time is anxiety?"

He strikes a chord. Not exactly what he wants.

Yvonne asks, "Jude have you been nipping this early?"

"No—I gave up drinking. I found it was just masking my symptoms. Now, I'm focusing on core issues—like asking, 'Why do I drink?' And, 'Why do I sometimes pretend I'm real?'"

"You aren't making a lot of sense. But not drinking will help."

Jude smirks. To the entire room he announces, "See? I'm right. If Mister MVP Joey Votto said what I did—they'd probably run the quote as the intro on ESPN's top show."

No one listens.

Jude went back to his meditation. In a micro-burst of enlightenment, he realizes *Joey Votto never said what's on the placard. Someone placed that saying there. How much of what we think and react to is just crap?* He says to the bobble-head, "I'm truly sorry, Joey."

Jude's phone buzzes.

He takes the call not knowing the identity of the caller, but upon hearing Matt's voice say, "Hello, Brother." he is immediately conflicted, by guilt for feeling shame over having a retarded-appearing brother, and joy at just having a brother.

"Uh...um....I....I...um..."

"Spit it out, Bro."

"Okay—It's just that I don't know what name I should call you. Are you Matthias, Matt, Otto—what?"

"Anything but *Tard* will do, *Brother.*"

"Ouch! I got it. I just want—"

Matt cut him off. "Skip it—this is not a family reunion. It's business."

"Business?"

"Yes, business."

"I don't understand. What kind of business?"

"Yours."

"Mine!? I—"

Matt's interruption is lightning quick. "Hellllloooo! Mars to Earth. Mars to Earth. Or, better yet—Matt to Bro. Matt to Bro."

"Now I'm really lost."

"Think, Jude—get your hungover-head out of your butt—I've been feeding you tips since the first week you called yourself a reporter. Hell, at times I even wrote your stories for you."

"Okay—okay, I *am* sorry. I *really* am. It's just that this whole thing has me….has me…"

"Has you what?"

"Confused—learning you are my brother. It's—it's—a little *unsettling*—to say the least."

"Actually, we are only half-brothers. So, cheer up. The gnome—you know, me—probably got his crap genes from outside your family. And if that doesn't soothe your nerves, count your blessings we never could have been twins."

Matt's tone breaks the ice—years of frozen, solid, hidden ice. Jude's ever-present anxiety for being a sodden disappointment to his sire, evaporates. His 'sins of the father' curse is gone—gifted to him by a new-found brother. No, half-brother. And one with a sense of humor…besides being Mystery Man of the Year.

"So, what is this *business*?"

"Your chance to be a hero—maybe."

"Me—a hero? This I've got to hear. I'm all ears, *Brother Matt.*"

* * *

MY FLYING-THING HAS ME HERE listening to plans, hopefully good ones that are aimed at rescuing me from terrible people doing even more terrible things.

I just can't go through anything like that again.

* * *

MATT QUICKLY EXPLAINS IN BRIEFER form what he had shared with Father Paul. Then he adds names—really just one.

"Remember Kyle Rattigan?"

"Sure, I'll never forget, Rat Rattigan. I heard he's in jail—doesn't surprise me—he's been in the trough of every wave for a long time."

"He's out of prison, back in town, and working at the Parker Home—that's why I need you to meet me there tonight at nine."

"You think he's probably involved in what the staff suspects?"

"The probability is not a probability at all. At least three staffers have told me he is *the cause* of it all."

"Are you one-hundred percent certain?"

"Yes. Remember all those leads and stories I spoon-fed you? All were golden—nothing but solid facts, with evidence, and witnesses."

"Point taken. I'll see you at nine."

"Brother......" Matt pauses for effect.

"Yeah?" Jude is pleased to be called 'Brother.'

Matt says emphatically, "Don't let me down."

A hurt-voice response comes back. "Man, that hurts. I mean really hurts."

"It was meant to. Richard needs the two of us. Just be there, Jude."

Matt ends the call.

---

* * *

THE CLOUD, THE DARKEST OF dark, is growing. My fear grows with it. My escape mechanism, my ability to fly, is seeping away from me. My anxiety and fear are growing, but I have two friends—brothers—who want to save me.

I only have them and my hope to fight the Darkness that is near.

ANOTHER PLAN

FORMER INMATE NUMBER 2573275 HAS been praised by the proponents of rehabilitation as an example of positive re-entry into society. They are wrong—not because they have made an error—they are wrong because he is not what they believe he is. He is not an ex-con. He is evil incarnate.

Rattigan sits in the employee lounge, 'the attending-medical-care-providers rest space,' as it was recently designated by the facility's HR department. He is musing over his plan to control the darkest elements of his home city and, most importantly, obtaining revenge on that *little freak bastard*.

He picks up his phone and initiates his plan.

"Snader—I've got a mission for you."

"Mission?"

"Yeah, it requires a man with what you have—a badge."

"Ra—I mean, Kyle. It better not be at the Parker Home."

"What's your beef?"

"I went to bat for you—remember? The Parker Home—"

Rattigan cuts him off.

"The Parker Home did shit—just like you. I got this suck-ass job because the lazy assholes in the HR office didn't bother to do a background check. They just look to be certain that a 'yes' box is checked when it has to be a yes. When everything is cool, they get another low-paid body to mop the puke and shit these so-called patients, really inmates, spew out of their sick decaying bodies. Who else would do that for the crap wages they pay? I'm here because no one else wants to be here. So, shut your pie-hole and listen."

Snader doesn't respond. What Rattigan said is true.

After a silence, Rattigan continues.

"We're filming a show tonight. We get paid very well by the pervs who go for the kind of stuff we produce. So, get your ass to Spitalfields—it's an art gallery. As a cop you ought to be able to find it. Flash your badge, get the chick, Mya, and bring her here at nine sharp tonight. Wait—make that earlier—eight-thirty. You can't miss her, she's an artsy type. *Do not* mess her up—no cuts, no bruises—her look is what I need. She's the new star of my next flick, but she doesn't know it yet. You got it?"

"No! I said no more—"

In a threatening voice, so close to Lucifer's own, Rattigan cuts him off again, "You better listen. If you don't do as I say, I'll send your boss, the D.A., your wife—and anybody else I can think of, a video of you with a jar of peanut butter and two very young girls. I'd say by their looks, they are five years under the jail-bait limit."

"No! You wouldn't—you can't." His words are meant to be strong. But they are hollow—very hollow—and Rattigan knows it.

Again, the voice from below speaks "Don't try me. If you do—I'll make sure my video goes viral. The world will be amazed at you finding uses and places for peanut butter. You have a gift you pedo-perv—and I got the video to prove it."

Silence again.

Rattigan waits to drive home his point. Hearing nothing, he closes the call with, "Good—pick up the star of the show. Be here a quarter to nine at the latest."

He pulls a cigar from his pocket, lights it up and triumphantly says, "I'm gonna ruin that little monkey through the people he cares for. And after I fill his life with pain, I'm going to own this fucking town."

Rattigan knows things about Snader and his friends.

They see themselves as the legacy of old-time hell-raisers when they are just lame losers playing at what I really do. If they were even the least bit like their role models, they'd know all human groups are run by people who know secrets, and the darker the secrets, the greater the control—and I know all of them.

* * *

THIS IS WHAT I WAS afraid of—the darkness I know as Rattigan. I am more afraid than I have ever been. I don't think I will be flying much anymore.

I may never fly again.

All I can do is pray Matt and Jude can save me.

* * *

THE SNATCH

ASSISTANT CHIEF SNADER, A SELF-PROCLAIMED mover-and-shaker in a group that hides its purpose, identity, and actions, sat in the alley behind Mya's art studio fretting over the threats of a greater presence of evil—Rattigan. He was fidgety and full of foreboding—a scared rabbit out of his hole.

Snader's mind raced. *This is madness. Rattigan is going off the rails. Abduction, kidnapping. Call it what you will, it's the last thing I need in my life. No—second to last thing. The first thing I do not need is that video going viral. Shit! Rattigan owns me.*

He checked his watch. *Eight. Five minutes to get the girl—fifteen, at most from here to Rattigan. Gives me at least ten as a buffer for any variables.* His concern was focused on meeting the demands of his taskmaster.

Snader exited his car, walked to the shop's rear door, and entered unannounced. Inside, he immediately encountered Miami, dressed in a 'slow-business-day' outfit.

Mildly surprised at the back-door entrance of a stranger, Miami asked loud enough for Mya to hear, "Can I help you?"

Reaching for his badge, Snader mumbled and fumbled, "Yeah—yeah...I—I —"

At that point he froze. Mind blank, he asked himself. *How could I forget? Who the fuck am I nabbing? Yeah—yeah—name starts with M. Arty look. Got to be her.*

Mid brain freeze, and before he could continue, Mya came in.

"Miami? Is everything okay?" she asked. Looking at Snader, Mya continued, "Hello. I'm Mya Krim, the owner. I'm sorry, but we are closed for the day."

Shit! Two Ms! Snader's brain went into overdrive. Remembering to flip his badge saved him. *I'll just take them both.* He flashed his credentials to both Ms.

He firmly said, "I'm not here to purchase art, or even to browse—I'm Assistant Chief Snader. The purpose of my coming is to have you accompany me to assist in an important matter." He knew he had them when they did not quickly push back. "If you need to take anything with you, such as a purse or whatever, please get them now and come with me."

Miami looked at Mya and shrugged her shoulders. Mya did the same. They then looked at Snader, who had assumed the stance of an authority figure.

Mya, regrouped a bit and politely asked, "How could the police need our help?"

Snader ignored her question and commanded, "Let's get moving, ladies. We need you for an identification. The need will be totally apparent soon. Let's go." He motioned toward the door. "My car is just outside."

In the car, Mya sensed things were off when Snader did not turn at the corner that would set the path to the police station. "Isn't that the turn for the station?"

Sander's reply was brief—very brief. "Yes, but you are needed elsewhere."

"Where are we going?"

Snader looked at his watch. He thought about his video and what Rattigan would do if he screwed up.

"Just relax. We're doing an ID at the Parker Home. It won't take long at all."

His answer calmed Mya's anxiety over the missed turn—some. But the fact their destination was the Parker Home was a troubling coincidence in light of what Matt had shared with her. She did not like the situation.

Snader caught her vibe. As he parked the car at their destination, he said with the slightest and most peculiar inappropriate-for-the-situation tone, "Ladies, this will be over quick—and maybe you'll even *enjoy* the experience."

The trio exited the car but did not go to the Parker Home's main entrance. Instead, the perverted corrupt cop guided Miami and Mya to an entrance nearest the hallway which lead to Richard's room. And a waiting rat, named Rat.

* * *

THE INCIDENT 2.0

I DON'T WANT TO BE HERE, but I can no longer fly away. Please do not stay. I don't want you to see what happens.

* * *

NADER OPENED THE DOOR AND motioned the two Ms to go in first. Miami entered without a thought. Mya hesitated. Her stationary time was short. Snader firmly pushed her forward. Her inner alarm went from caution to full alert.

"What's this about? Really?" She began to turn-about to confront Snader, but he shoved her into the hallway.

"You'll find out soon." Snader pushed her and Miami, until both women were at the door of the nearest room. He tapped on the door and called out, "We're here." The door opened. Snader forced the women into the room.

Shocked by the treatment, disoriented by entering the building through a side door, Mya was surprised to find they were in Richard's room. Her anxiety turned into full-blown fear upon recognition of Kyle Rattigan, whose immediate intention was displayed when he lashed out at Snader.

"You fucking idiot. Why did you bring two?"

A cowering Snader covered his incompetence and sought to explain, "I—I—I didn't know who was who. Their names are similar—so I brought them both."

His answer was accepted by Rattigan. Thinking. Scheming. An augmented plan.

"Okay. Maybe it's better...for the film." He ominously grinned. "There's a strong market for three-ways." He looked at the two women as a slave buyer would at an auction. "Yeah...this might be better. Sure—sure—much better."

The details escaped her, but Miami understood. She and her boss were in a bad situation and all she could do was tremble. Rattigan observed her help- lessness and grinned. She was totally in his control.

In the past Rattigan had used hidden cameras for blackmail purposes, but now he had a studio-quality camera set up. Upon seeing it, Mya deduced enough of his plan to explode. She rushed toward him. "Kyle Rattigan, you sick bastard. You'll have to kill us to—"

Rattigan grabbed her throat and placed a gun directly between her eyes, stopping her cold.

"Don't move. You fucking bitch. You better not say another word."

Mya trembled like Miami. He shoved her to Snader and barked, "Sit both of 'em on the floor against the wall—Now!"

Again, Snader did as he was told.

When the women were placed as he had directed, Rattigan instructed Snader.

"Here..." He gave Snader a bottle of clear liquid and surgical sponges.

"What's this?"

"Chloroform."

"You want to knock them out? I thought—"

"Stop thinking. Just give 'em enough to slow them down for a couple minutes."

Yet again, Snader complied. Uncapping the bottle and pouring the contents on a sponge, he placed the second sponge near the bottle, but forgot to recap the bottle. In less than two minutes, both Mya and Miami were listless and nearly unconscious.

A syringe and small bottle next appeared out of Rattigan's pocket. Snader did not ask a thing. He, too, was under Rattigan's control.

"This is why I wanted them asleep," Rat explained. "It's impossible to shoot someone up when they are fighting and squirming."

Pointing to the bottle, Snader asked, "What's in it?"

"My special mix. When they come to, they'll be compliant to instructions, as well as being awake enough to be filmed. No one will buy a flick with a zombie sucking and fucking. It looks phony." He grinned like a fiend about to commit a relished atrocity.

"An absolutely brilliant plan—love it." Snader grinned a lesser version of Rattigan's grin. He fully approved of being controlled.

"You'll like it even more when you join the fun. Not too old for your taste, are they?"

"They'll do." Still grinning, Snader asked, "When does my fun start?"

"You shoot 'em up. We wait about fifteen minutes, they eat salami—then they're yours. And, don't worry, I promise not to film your face."

Snader bound Miami's arm, preparing her for a shot. He drew some of the contents from the small bottle and injected her arm. Almost immediately, she entered into a seizure, violently jerked and coughed a foamy blend of saliva and blood out onto her chest.

"What the fuck?" Rattigan screamed. "What did you do? How much did you use?" He frantically shook Miami, then Snader, and back to Miami.

Snader blabbered, "I don't—I don't know—I'm not a doctor. Don't blame me. Maybe your mixture is too powerful."

"Check her pulse—see if she's dead," yelled Rattigan.

Snader could not move, overwhelmed by the event..

Impatient to know the level of damage done, Rattigan shoved Snader away from the slumped over Miami.

"Fuck! Do I have to do everything myself?" Rattigan grabbed Miami's wrist and felt for a sign of life. "Good! She's not dead. If she wakes up soon enough, we'll still get some use out of her."

Snader had not moved. Rattigan had forcefully pushed him aside causing Snader's foot to topple the chloroform bottle. He had hit the wall and slid down into the pooled chloroform face-first. Snader was unconscious in seconds.

Rattigan yelled, "Shit! Shit! Shit!"

Of course, there was no reply from the three corpse-like forms—the products of his creation.

* * *

JUDE ARRIVED AT THE PARKER Home a few minutes before nine. He looked around and saw no activity. *The place is a ghost town. Doesn't look like a hotbed of criminal activity.*

Maybe— He was interrupted by a tap on the passenger window.

"I'm glad you made it. I'm *really* glad," Matt said. He flashed a smile so beautiful Jude believed in family once again. "Come on in with me to check for secret cameras, I need your height to peek above and behind the cabinets and in the top corners of the ceiling. We need to get a ladder for the check light fixtures—janitor's closet should have one."

"Do you think anything will be there?"

"I paid a hundred to a snitch that says he helped Rattigan install at least one camera."

"Can you really trust that information?"

"Maybe," replied Matt. "That's why we are here. This is a do-it-yourself project. If we find what I suspect is here, the info goes to my favorite reporter— any guess who that might be?"

"Okay, I'm with you—lead the way."

They entered the Parker Home through the front entrance and approached the reception desk center-left in the small lobby. No one was present. In fact, no one in control, a supervisory role or in a plain work mode of any sort, was available.

"Good, it's a ghost town outside and a morgue in here," Jude said. "We won't be bothered poking around here—the place is empty." He was soon to be proved wrong. Very wrong.

Matt pointed to one of three hallways to exit the lobby, and said, "This one on the left leads to where we're headed, number twelve, last one on the right nearest the side door. That's Richard's room."

"How long has he been here?"

"Just after the day that ruined his life. And, if I'm correct in what is going on here, the horror of Rattigan is visiting upon him again. Exploitive stuff—very sick, as I explained. Let's get moving."

They headed down the hall.

On the way, when they came upon a men's room, Jude said, with a twinge of embarrassment, "I want to make a stop—pee break. I'll catch up. Room twelve—right?"

"Yeah, twelve."

"I'll see you there in a few."

Matt proceeded alone to Richard's room where a scurrying Rat moved bodies.

Countless times Matt had opened the door to Richard's room. He sometimes found one of the staff, cleaning, administering care to his friend, or nodded off in his reading chair. Most often he found nothing beyond Richard appearing to be asleep.

Having seen no staff up front, he assumed they were 'ghosting' their supervisors, or having a longer than routine smoke break.

As Matt opened the door, he heard scuffling sounds. His antennae immediately signaled danger.

When the door opened, Rattigan was caught lugging an unconscious Snader away from the of aim of the camera. A disheveled Miami had already been moved, and Mya was propped against the foot of Richard's bed.

"What the fuck?" blurted Rattigan, as he looked over his shoulder at the intruder to his scheme. He dropped Snader and spun about to attack.

"Mya!" Matt yelled.

Rattigan pounced.

Size and weight difference, plus enraged energy landed Rattigan directly on the object of his revenge. Matt did not have a chance at any defense, and was propelled against the door frame, striking it with tremendous force.

Still conscious, Matt attempted to remain standing, but was racked with excruciating pain. His face reddened as he clutched his chest.

Heart attack.

Matt blacked out.

I awoke.

* * *

WHEN MY ABILITY TO FLY totally left me, I was certain it was due to the closeness and growing strength of the dark cloud. But I was wrong—so very wrong. I believe it was not the dark, but the goodness of life keeping me in my room. Making it impossible for me to flee from a moment in time when I had to act.

On many occasions when Matt read to me, I was close to waking up and joining him. I never made it. But at this time of crisis, I broke the bindings holding me. I crossed a line and exited my coma. I was there—awake and able to make choices in the here and now. Not in a fantasy. And not as a peeping Tom. I could act.

And I did.

It is very troubling and terrible to partake of violence—even to observe it. I do not like violence in any form—just consider my circumstances and how they arrived.

I remember being confused when Matt read the Bible to me. Violence is in many of its old stories. They are full of it. But violence is complicated, and permissible as when applied as justice, defense of self, home, the innocent—that's Good Guy violence. Even Jesus lashed out, using violence to punish evil doers when he scourged the money changers materially profiting from the spiritual beliefs of the innocent.

It was my turn. I awoke with one thought, *Thou shalt not be a victim, and thou shalt not be a perpetrator. But above all else—thou shalt not be a bystander.*

My mentor had imbued in me through all his readings, his talks, and even his jokes that, opposite from its nature, Love can properly use violence.

I got out of the bed that had been my prison for years, grabbed the reading lamp and swung it with all the energy my body could draw upon. Fueled by a righteous brand of adrenalin, I responded by choosing to deliver justice.

Rattigan never saw it coming, nor did he have a chance at survival.

I'm not proud of what I did. It was an immoral act—the most final—performed for moral reasons. In defense of the innocent a perpetrator of evil was vanquished. Case closed.

Then I collapsed.

***

A S A REPORTER, JUDE HAD experienced many after-violence sites. That night, he expected to enter Room 12 to find Matt waiting for assistance in their mission to discover evidence. Instead, he walked into a scene of chaos and mayhem. His mind immediately went to work.

He surveyed the room—five bodies, cameras, blood, the smell of chloroform, and drug paraphernalia clearly in sight. He quickly checked pulses, assessed each person's condition, and with speed and clarity of mind, surmised the situation in a manner which would indeed make Sherlock Holmes envious.

Then he took further action. Action with high potential to land him in jail.

Avoiding splatters, Jude positioned Rattigan next to the still unconscious Snader, and placed the chloroform bottle near the two of them. Next, he propped Mya and Miami up and against the wall. He then wrapped his hand in a handkerchief, grabbed the syringe and small bottle, and slipped them into Snader's pocket.

Next, Jude laid me back on my bed. In lifting and putting me on the bed, I experienced a new and very unfamiliar consciousness. Jude noticed, looked into my eyes for a reaction, and quired, "You okay, big fella?"

After years of not speaking, I croaked in a whisper, "Okay—take care of your brother."

Jude calmly assured me, a stressed-out patient, "Don't worry, Richard, I will." He grinned and gave a conspirator-like wink. "I need to do a couple more things and then he's on his way to the Emergency Room."

With the same handkerchief from before, he wiped my fingerprints off the lamp, and placed the lamp in Snader's hand, being certain a new set of prints was made.

His final cover-up act was to scan the scene. When satisfied with his efforts, Jude carried his stricken brother out of the room.

* * *

AFTERMATH AND AFTER MATT

ETTING A BODY TO AND into an auto is not as easy as it sounds. The dead or unconscious weigh more. For some unknown Law of the Universe, dead weight always acts as if it is double its actual amount. Lugging a corpse-like body around is one matter, dealing with Matt when he revived was another.

Matt awoke in pain, head-strong, and critical. He refused to go to the hospital. And he meant it.

"Jude—listen to me. I *cannot* go to *any* emergency room. As far as the medical system is concerned, I'm a ghost. All my records are hand-written, with no copies, and they are all with Claudia Marconi. Any tests she has done on me are under fake names. That's how we've kept me hidden. My privacy is all I have."

Matt's statement was his 'I'm-digging-my-heels-in' explanation of the situation, delivered at half his normal voice level. It was obvious he had experienced a major assault on his weak heart.

Jude's concern was real and urgent. "Matt, you've had a heart attack. This is serious." *Damn! I've just found that I have a brother, an amazing one. Now that very individual, genius that he is, wants to…to…what?*

Jude did ask, "Matt *what* do you want to do? If you don't go the E.R. you could die." He stared at Matt in bewilderment. "*What*? Tell me."

"Take me to my place. Call Claudia—have her meet us there."

Jude set a course to Matt's sanctuary on Water Street. As they pulled out of the parking lot, Jude called Claudia at home. Claudia asked for symptoms and Jude gave the details.

By way of speakerphone, Claudia spoke to Matt, "I know you won't listen to me, but I have to try. Matt, you need to go to the E.R. Now!"

"No way, Doc. It's my place or nothing."

* * *

JUDE GOT THEM TO WATER Street in minutes, put Matt immediately onto the bed, and made two calls. The first was 911.

"Nine-one-one—what is the nature of your emergency?"

Sounding urgent, afraid, and in a hoarse voice, Jude replied, "A terrible thing happened at the Parker Home, Room Twelve. I think someone is dead." He quickly ended the call.

His second call was to Marty Wall, a colleague who was an old-school TV reporter with bloodhound DNA in his veins. Marty instantly recognized Jude's voice, but before he could utter a greeting, Jude started, "Don't say a word, Marty. You never got this call—just get your butt and a camera man to Room Twelve at the Parker Home as fast as possible. It's the best story in your career—trust me."

Marty quipped a peremptory excuse for if he ever got caught, "I have no idea who you are and no clue why you are bothering me."

Jude responded, "Love ya, Dude—hope you get an Emmy."

With that done, all Jude could do was keep Matt comfortable and wait.

When Claudia arrived, she immediately went to work as best she could.

"Matt, to accurately diagnose the damage you've sustained, I need an EKG. Also, an IV drip with the appropriate medications is required."

The response from Matt was the same. "I need to be here for reasons which you are well aware. Get what you need, but I'm staying here. If there is something I should have that can't be brought to me, I'll just have to get by without it."

"Matt, you *should* be in the telemetry unit at Lancaster General now—not here."

"I'm *not* going anywhere. End of discussion."

* * *

MARTY WALL ARRIVED AT ROOM 12 only seconds behind the 911 first responders. Soon, every cop in the county was on-site in some form or fashion. Patrol units, crime scene investigators, and homicide detectives crowded in and around Room 12. Complete pandemonium allowed Marty an even greater on-the-scene access than normal, and that night Marty delivered his career best performance.

Quickly, the narrative of a dirty cop surviving a deadly fight with his convicted-felon partner during an abduction-porn filming was the best explanation for a dead Rattigan, an unconscious Snader, with drugs and paraphernalia found on him, and two kidnapped drugged women prepped for a filming. The reason for the specific location, and Richard's potential participation, was delicately explained. There was zero mention of Jude and Matt ever having been associated with what happened.

Details of the event were the talk of the town. It went viral.

The news story was as good as anything in a movie or a program on TV. Kidnapping, murder, sex videos, corruption, blackmail—a sordid tale made for gossip.

And, when the real and staged pieces were put together, the narrative was a slam-dunk for the city's prosecutors.

Snader's fingerprints nailed him for Rattigan's murder, and the testimonies of Mya and Miami confirmed him as their abductor. Rattigan's past, revealed in the testimony of key Parker Home staff and the video setup explained the overall intent for the perverted crime they were about to film. Especially titillating, were the rumors concerning Snader's video, the one Rattigan held over his head. It seemed there were several other prominent community leaders appearing as The Peanut Butter Bunch.

If possible, it got worse for Snader after a bizarre note was found in his wallet. A devotee of sickness of the worst kind, Snader kept a quote purported to be from The Son of Sam on him at all times.

It read: HELLO FROM THE GUTTERS OF WHICH ARE FILLED WITH DOG MANURE, VOMIT, STALE WINE, URINE AND BLOOD. HELLO FROM THE SEWERS OF WHICH SWALLOW UP THESE DELICACIES WHEN THEY ARE WASHED AWAY BY THE SWEEPER TRUCKS.

The repercussions of the event traveled at warp speed. Several senior managers at the Parker Home were sacked and the owners were very nervous, about not only the facilities reputation, but liability for such activities taking place within the walls of their business. Government inspectors and lawsuits loomed on the horizon. Scandal fed frenzy. It was something to experience—the hypnotic-compulsive spell was similar to a car-crash sucking observers into its web of control. Add the sordid elements, such as a fallen cop, drugs, sex, etc., with the media, and what you got was a gawkers' feast. The only thing to end it was the limited attention span of the public, which may be even the greater scandal.

A week later, everything was back to what passed as normal. Abnormal? Routine? Plain old life? The news, and public interest focused upon the next *Big Story*, which was followed by another one, and the one after that.

In the shuttling and scuffling of the collective unconscious zeitgeist, or 'the system' which is mysteriously controlled by the unidentified ghost-like *They*, no one really cared, and importantly, no one noticed Matt—a non-player in it all. He was healing and hiding out in the same manner as always—in plain sight.

On the second floor of a garage-type building, in a small apartment, a dwarfish little man slept much less than normal folk, but more than his usual. He took pills and tidied up the affairs of his life—the one which had gone on without notice while exerting massive influence for the general good.

Matt did not—could not—visit me. We had no wondrous reunion. Matt's condition limited his mobility, and even after my 'miraculous' recovery I was still imprisoned at the Parker Home.

Father Paul, with the considered medical opinion of Claudia to fortify his efforts, toiled daily in the swamp-like environs of the state bureaucracy to obtain my recognition as being something other than mentally disabled and forever forced to remain as a ward of an indifferent incompetent authority.

They marveled at my physical recovery and were confounded by my mental capacities. However, the response of the ruling *Theys* was to boldly commission a study—a safe drop back—and punt me into a non-solution.

When embroiled in the endless frustrating task of freeing me, Father Paul was often heard muttering, "All of this is bullshit" so many times each day that the untrained ear might support the notion the Orthodox priest had converted and had chosen a five-word mantra to prove it.

For me, my new existence was a seemingly endless amount of physical therapy. The freedom of my flying was replaced by the realization I had spent years in a bed. Muscles had atrophied, bed sores had appeared, healed, and reappeared. Lumps of scar tissue marred me.

Matt's almost nightly visits, where he assisted in keeping me as healthy as possible, had postponed much of the inevitable ills of being me. But now awake, I faced the task of sitting, standing, and walking. The adrenalin of awakening was long gone. Balance was an important word. Gravity was another. The defense of my friends from Rattigan, never an assault in my mind, had been fueled by one of those miracles. Truly, a one-off event.

I was back in the *real world*. I had to build a new body. But all I could think of was Matt's recovery, not mine.

I asked Father Paul, "When can I see Matt?" as many times a day as he chanted his mantra for my freedom.

"Soon. Soon," Father Paul told me. "Focus on your health. Claudia will focus on his."

And, Father Paul prayed—much more than he said his mantra. He suggested I pray, too. Also, he reminded me the prayer line, our personal communication channel to the heavens, was open twenty-four-seven, three-hundred sixty-five days a year, at no cost.

I could no longer fly. So, I placed my desires in words—and they flew upward. I cast my seeds upon the Universe hoping they would take root and grow. But my prayers were not answered.

One day Matt just disappeared.

* * *

MATT'S DEPARTURE WAS UNANNOUNCED. TOTALLY gone. Devastating. A clean break.

Jude lost his new-found brother, Father Paul could no longer debate his shadow conscience, Claudia could not be tested and challenged as a healer. Their world was darker without Matt. All were sad.

I, earthbound, weak, lonely, soon to be free, had lost everything.

* * *

An End is My Beginning

ON MY FIRST DAY OUT in the world I met the others at Matt's home. From what Jude could deduce everything within the man-cave that served as the home of a genius was as it should be. Matt's books, stereo, pipes, artwork, computers, papers—everything—was the same as always.

Only Matt was gone.

The reason for our meeting lay on his desk, the place where Otto Janus penned the vastly popular and financially successful series of mysteries. Clues? Signposts? His journal was in the waste can, burnt to ashes. On the desk, placed above the ashes of his life, sat four envelopes. Our names were written on them in his distinct hand.

"I haven't touched them," Jude told us. "I felt that he would have liked the four of us to gather like this."

Claudia asked, "Did any of you have an inkling about this? Because I am blindsided. My routine visit yesterday was routine. There was no hint of him going anywhere."

Father Paul and Jude also professed they had no idea about Matt's plans. They were equally shocked by Matt's surprise departure.

Me—I had been praying just to see him again.

We took our envelopes. Father Paul opened his first. Inside was a sizable cashier's check and a note with two brief messages. Father Paul's eyes misted at the end of the first message.

He looked at us and said, "It's Matt's instructions for the money—he penned his own version of Jesus instructing his followers on how the greatest one among them should wash the feet of his lessors. You know, 'the first shall be last'." Father Paul did not read the exact words. He wept instead.

The second message? It was not shared either. Later, I found that it contained instructions on how Father Paul could access an account for my care— with the wish the end of my wardship would be within six months. Matt wanted me to quickly become independent and 'find my way'.

Mya's envelope also contained two parts. First, was a check providing funds for her to follow her artistic inspirations without depending upon her shop's success. Second, there was research on the Parker Home's ownership and enough funds for her and Miami to engage a suit to receive compensation for their ordeal. Matt wanted justice for the Home's neglect in hiring Rattigan and fostering the environment for him to conduct his evils upon the innocent.

Matt reversed Occam's Razor—the law that explains, when encountering a number of solutions for a problem, the simplest answer is the correct one. In assisting Mya and Miami, Matt was employing his variation—Occam's Safety Razor, in which the simplest answer to exposing a CYA effort was to expose the deception being played out by the nefarious and greedy.

Mya was overwhelmed. Yet, she was very uncomfortable I was not mentioned in the strategy. She said I, too, had been wronged and she begged me to be part of the legal action.

I said, "No." Matt had other plans for me—I just felt it.

Matt's farewell to Jude was different—more elaborate and mysterious. Jude's message read:

Ride the wave my brother, remembering you cannot control it. Become able to ignore its hollow message. Every human is responsible to and for every other human, accountable only to the Creator. I believe we can make a better world one person at a time. You be the start. Be the hero I know you can be. Peace and love from your brother, Matthias.

Also, in that envelope was a portable computer drive. Its information, containing instructions and support messages to Jude, covered use of the majority of Matt's hidden resources. The core of his stocks, bonds, CDs and land that originally came from Otto Janus's book royalties. The remainder was Matt's proceeds from outsmarting those who claimed to be wheeler-dealers on Wall Street.

In following Matt's instructions, Jude soon established The Janus Foundation and began dispersing Matt's wealth to good causes. For the foundation's motto, Jude selected a statement he remembered from one of Matt's books: MEND WITH THE HEART THAT WHICH HAS BEEN INJURED BY HANDS AND MINDS IN MISGUIDED SERVICE TO THE DESIRE FOR MORE.

Matt's most important instructions, especially for Jude, were steps for revealing the identity of the reclusive author, Otto Janus. Matt intended that Jude would be revealed as the actual Otto Janus.

Matt was gone, but even in exile or death, he was positive in his deceptions. I believe, through Jude, he was inverting the occult Picatrix, the ancient four-hundred-page text said to be the handbook of talismanic magic. Some called it the cookbook on how to be bad. Matt liked to reverse bad to good. Was he creating a modern positive version of the Picatrix's goal by making Jude the guinea pig on how to be the best possible human? I'd bet so.

Upon learning that a much-praised award-winning journalist was the mystery man of popular literature, it was possible for Jude to transform himself, as Otto Janus, into a full-time writer. Quickly, he announced the Amish detective series was over and that he would develop new projects.

Between religiously attending AA meetings and promoting rehabilitation assistance for alcohol and drug abusers, Jude, AKA Otto Janus, produced the first in a new line of books aimed at a young audience. First, he exposed to the world the insightful and entertaining morality tales of *Freddie the Fox* and his friends and followed up with more tales of good versus evil. Jude had found his purpose.

And then there was my envelope.

Without Matt my life was empty. Now Me had no opportunity to tell him about my flying adventures. There was no opportunity to say hello. There had been no goodbye.

* * *

I Do Not Like This

Now awake, I am a fully developed newborn. My brain is filled with the equivalent of a lifetime of reading—all the good stuff—the *really* good stuff. For most of my life, I have been a ward of the state, an ignorant structure run by incompetent, greedy, ambitious apparatchiks who possess no conception of who I am, what I can accomplish, or how I came to be. They do not care. Matt did, but he is gone.

If people are honest, they maybe have a few true friends, or two or three. Some have none. I had Matt. And now, he is gone. Without him, I feel lost.

As I look at my new world, I do not like what I see. There is no meaningful discussion of anything. It's all buy and sell, sell and buy. In politics, a liar will say, "Elect me! I will save you from the last liar who said, 'Elect me!'" Teachers declare, "Statistics lie—and I have the statistics to prove it," as they rush to attend a union meeting to pad their pensions.

The world I see is a dystopian hell. My peers have no higher functions. No intellectual life. No interests or hobbies. There is no conversation, just social media—full of dismissive one-liners with no depth or background. There is little faith-in anything—except self-presentation.

How many *likes* do you think I'll get for saying that?

More people believe in aliens, the little green men type, than in God.

A popular athlete's daughter being arrested for drug possession is news.

Someone paid nine million dollars for the website porn.com—without any content—just the name.

Bizarre gawking is rife on TV, with shows such as *Obese And Pregnant* being followed by the *One Ton Family*, and *Jersey Shore*.

One quarter of surveyed young people stated they would replace a lover with an android. Illogically warped thinking prevails everywhere. Much of it is camouflaged by well-intended ideals, such as caring for the disadvantaged—which, in reality, means anyone who had not gotten what *they* want—as opposed to providing what is really needed for authentic improvement of our society. It is true the road to Hell is paved with good intentions.

I have found myself in a world in which, "Where is my smart phone?" is the epitome of curiosity. That's the bottom of the heap. But it is no better at the top where Andy Warhol's prediction of everyone being famous for fifteen minutes is played out by the most privileged of the herd, grabbing their quarter-hour in the spotlight by way of a self-indulgent TED Talk—with wine and cheese followed by the obligatory, near-compulsory, book signing and selfie opportunity.

I am repulsed by TV news. Recently a marginally reputable newscaster covered, with faux seriousness, the arrest of a woman dressed in a Sumo wrestler suit who assaulted her ex-boyfriend in a pub after he waved hello to another woman dressed as a *Snickers* bar. What can one expect when people kill one another to preserve life in an age which prefers the sign to the thing signified, the copy to the original, the appearance to essence? In my new world, illusion is sacred, truth has become profane.

If I am overreacting, based upon my experience when the gang abused me that fateful day, it is to be expected. We live in a world of, "My dog ate my decency." Sadly, the gang of children who tortured me has grown up, their Halloween world is now very real and they are in charge.

I like animals as much as most people do. But maybe we need to take a breather when an animal rights organization launches a Lobster Empathy Program in an old jail to demonstrate how lobsters are imprisoned prior to execution. People have always been peculiar, but that excuse might also be accompanied by some basic sane pursuits—like halting the activities of humans mistreating humans.

Not engaging in war would be a nice start. Abolishing the death penalty? "Pick your poison" is not a joke—it's a lifestyle—or a sick execution choice.

There is no cure. This brave new world is one full of addictions sprinkled with confetti. Alcohol. Sex. Food. Drugs. Relevance. Ignorance. Celebrity.

Botox and plastic surgery do not work on culture. On the celeb issue, one thought—in the vein of the Amish-farm-wisdom Matt told me, "Celebrity worship is akin to flies swarming a manure pile."

Religion? You cannot rely on organized humans. Structure is not spirit. Religion has a choke-hold on the soul and only offers a placebo overdose.

Simply, people are not good to each other. There is no material answer to a spiritual problem, and merely organizing the material one way or another is of little use even when the intent is noble.

There is no benefit to *Wokeness* in a spiritual wasteland, and the answer will not appear if the right question is never asked. I yearn for less when all about me clamber for *more*.

Often, I find myself praying about problems which have no correlation but their emptiness.

I cry out Matt's simple prayer, "Dear God, please forgive me. Teach me truth. Guide me home. Send angels to help me see your kingdom."

* * *

CLAUDIA EXPLAINED TO ME MATT had been very sick. Sicker than just a heart attack. Facing the inevitable presented him with the choice of how best to aid those he cared for. I think Matt wanted to avoid everything to do with the end as others saw it.

Matt, benign knowing observer, true master of a lesser world, utilized his superiority—that of being an enlightened outcast. He set up Jude and pointed him in a direction—one that would be good for him, and many others.

The same with Father Paul—providing him with ample resources to do spiritual good in a material world.

For Mya, not being Matt's life-partner was an ever-present heart-pain for them both. His absence set her free of the want they could never have. He made it possible for her to fill that void with art and creativity.

For me, it was a new life filled with the challenge to find meaning.

For himself? He disappeared for good, making it impossible for the state, the system, or anyone else, to latch on to him and study him as an oddity—destroying his freedom.

Matt's illness made him less able to fight against the nameless, faceless paper-pushing bureaucrats who made decisions when they had no skin in the game.

He feared very little, but he was very aware of the damage their incompetent indifference could create.

He wrote about that, too.

* * *

THE SIDEWALK TO NOWHERE

by Otto Janus

THE BAILIFF'S VOICE SLICED THROUGH the verbal clutter which hung like mist above the crowd. "All rise." he commanded.

Mumbling stopped, chairs squeaked, and bodies groaned as the human contents of the courtroom stood in obedience. A tiny smile, fueled by temporary authority, flicked across the bailiff's lips.

He continued, "The Court of Mansfield County, State of Pennsylvania, the Honorable Judge Claire Pickering presiding is now in session."

A slight, silver-haired woman of advanced years entered. Silent, without looking up from her papers, using some form of internal radar, the judge eased toward a chair behind the bench, and upon finding her target, was abruptly sucked downward by gravity. In silence, the assembly remained standing.

Clearing her throat, Judge Pickering eyed the room and ordered, "Be seated."

The room sighed. Its contents reclined.

The judge peered over her papers. To the prosecutor, a man of impeccable grooming, she said, "Mr. Perry. I see that the first case is the State versus William Greene."

Jason Perry, the prosecutor, still standing at near attention, said, "Yes, your Honor, the first item on the docket is State versus Greene, third-class felony assault upon a public servant."

"Greene—Greene—William Greene," muttered the judge. "Why do I remember that name?" She answered her own question with a question. Looking up, the judge aimed her sight away from the prosecutor to where the defense attorney and defendant should be located.

Her eyes rested upon an average man of average looks, average height and in his mid-years standing alone. "Weren't you the source of all the ruckus about that sidewalk?"

"I am," answered the man.

"Where's your attorney?"

"I don't want one."

"It's, '*Your Honor*'," schooled the bailiff. His instruction was accompanied by the fiercest stink-eye stare he could muster.

Greene eyeballed the bailiff in return. He slowly repeated, "I said I don't want a lawyer."

Before the bailiff could respond, the judge waved him back. She admonished Greene herself. "You're not starting out very well, Mr. Greene," began the lecture. "In my courtroom you'll find it advantageous to have both an attorney and a proper attitude."

"No offense intended, Judge Pickering. It's a point with me. Titles are okay, but I'm only inclined to honor or respect someone after they've earned it."

It was the judge's opportunity to stink-eye—if she chose. She did not. Instead, she pivoted back to her earlier position of familiarity with Greene. "Am I correct in assuming your appearance here today is linked to your fight against the Planning Commission's sidewalk regulations?"

"Yes," Greene answered. He offered no more. But she wanted more.

"How?" Judge Pickering asked, making a *come hither* sign with her fingers.

Before an answer could come, Jason Perry interrupted.

"Your Honor. As Prosecutor, I feel compelled to object. This is an arraignment hearing, with no plea entered and—"

Judge Pickering cut him off with an abrupt wave of her hand. He ignored it and persisted.

"Your Honor, I—"

She halted him again, this time with a summons. "Mr. Perry—approach the bench." Perry defiantly complied by walking slowly and casually forward.

Judge Pickering was not amused. In a low whisper, Claire Pickering informed him of her displeasure.

"Look here, Jason. I may be retiring next week, but it is more than enough time for me to toss your nuts in a grinder. Instead of one day sitting in this seat, you'll be down the hall overseeing parking tickets and judging the hot dog eating contest at the county fair. Got me?"

"Yes," he whispered back.

"What?" she hissed.

"Yes, Your Honor. I'm so sorry. I—"

She cut him off again.

"This is my courtroom. If I want to talk to *any-one* in it—I will. And, procedure be damned. When you're a judge—and I having my doubts if you ever will be—you'll understand." With a flick of her hand, she dismissed him. As he turned, she whispered her final instructions. "Go sit down and shut up."

Turning, she said, "Now, Mr. Greene, please—tell me about the sidewalk and how it got you here."

The defendant smiled and said, "Yes, *Your Honor*, I'm pleased to."

The judge smiled back.

Greene continued, "I've run Greene Motors on Highway Nineteen since my father died thirty years ago. Nuthin' fancy—just good running cars and trucks at fair prices. We do repairs, also. That's how we stay in business—we fix what we sell—stand behind the vehicles. Never been in court over anything—sales or repairs."

"That's admirable, very admirable," Judge Pickering commented.

Perry groaned ever so slightly. He sat up stiff and stared to the side when Claire looked his way.

"Please continue."

"About a year ago I decided to repave our lot. The estimate was near thirty-two thousand dollars. That's a lot for a small business, but I said, 'What the heck—been making do with patches for more than twenty years—it's time for an upgrade.' So, I went ahead got the worked scheduled with Jake Bemis and his crew and that's when the trouble started."

The judge leaned forward. "How so?"

"Regulations—tons of 'em. Years ago, when we first paved the lot—we just paved it. Now, it's become a nightmare." Greene shifted his weight from side-to-side in an expression of agitation. "Jake Bemis tells me I have to get a permit. It's my lot, but I can't put a layer of asphalt on my old asphalt without the county's say so. So, I file for a permit. Costs me time *and* money. Then I learn I can't get a permit without a plan—one that is drawn by a highway architect and okayed by a highway engineer. When I go to the architect, he explains that the newest regulations say I have to add a sidewalk."

"The sidewalk to nowhere—right?"

"Yes!" Greene became more animated. "We're on Highway Nineteen. Dead in the middle of a stretch where there's nothing but fields, us, then more fields. The nearest anything is six-hundred yards in either direction from our entrance. Why do we need a sidewalk?"

He looked to the judge for an answer, and she gave him a blank stare.

Greene continued. "Exurbia. That's what they call it."

He was on a roll.

"Planners dream up names like that for expansion and sprawl just to make it sound like they know what they're doing. But they don't."

"I understand you protested the sidewalk?"

"Oh, yes. But it got me nowhere just like the darn thing itself. In the end, I had to add a sidewalk—one that nobody will ever walk on. It starts nowhere and goes nowhere."

"Truly the sidewalk to nowhere," commented the judge.

"Yes! And in the end, it cost me thirteen thousand dollars more than the original estimate, plus the plan and the architect."

"Now I understand your campaign of letters to the editor and the signs you posted. I remember seeing them. The newspaper gave you a good amount of coverage. I guess that's why I could readily recall your name."

"The paper was decent. I have to give them that. But the first part is probably not what you remember."

"So...Mr. Greene," the judge smiled. "I sense the sidewalk wasn't the end of it. How did you end up here, today, with this serious charge?"

"You're right, it was not the end. There was more—a lot more."

"There always is. Proceed."

"Not a day after the cement dried, I got a notice it had to be redone."

"Why?"

"Handicap access. The bureaucrats went retro on me. They said the plans I submitted had only been approved 'in concept' and I had to re-do the sidewalk to meet handicap access requirements. That's the fight you remember. I made a stink—especially after Jim Cornwell was hit by a car while trying to remove concrete and set new molds for the handicap access."

"A man was injured?"

"Worse. Jim was horribly injured—crippled, in fact. All for a sidewalk no one will ever use—let alone use in a wheelchair. He's a simple guy, but what a worker. Jim's at least sixty, has no benefits, is raising a set of grandkids, and now he's crippled. I paid his hospital bill. The church has helped. Friends, family, all the folks who know him pitched in. But, the local bureaucrats—the same idiots who caused the situation to occur in the first place—the real culprits? They let him down. They 'lost his claim' for assistance."

"That's horrendous."

"Damn right it is. And when I was in the county office trying to get things sorted out for Jim, a fat office boy quipped that Jim had 'fallen through a crack in the sidewalk to nowhere.' That's when I lost it and socked that S.O.B. as hard as I could. So,

Your Honor, I won't need a lawyer. I plead guilty to helpin' and defendin' my fellow man. I guess you could call me a misdirected, but well-intended, Good Samaritan. Throw the book at me if you want, but I had to help my neighbor. The bad part was my losing it over that fat turd's comment."

The judge sighed heavily. She stink-eyed the prosecutor and waited for him to do the right thing.

Visibly cowed, he nodded in silent obedience.

In almost a whisper, he said, "Your Honor, Prosecution moves for dismissal."

* * *

MATT HATED VIOLENCE, BUT HE believed in righteous justice—and if it required a blow or a smack in the face to right a wrong, or make a statement—he was okay that it be applied.

The Incident was one such example.

My awakening was another. I think he expressed that in this last story.

Matt is not here to guide me through the process of addressing my guilt of taking a life, but he taught me much. And, he pointed me in a direction.

Can the three words he left me be enough?

I have to find my way—The Way—and I have to do it on my own.

* * *

ONE BLESSING OF WAKING UP in these times is that people's attention spans are about as long as their memory of the last TV commercial they saw.

My miraculous awakening did not produce the much-touted fifteen minutes of fame for me, and for that I am happy. In this technology-driven diminished-attention-span culture, I thankfully received less than five seconds of notice and zero fame. I was a blip on the radar screen. The good side of my situation is no one recalls the Then Me and my stupendous mental advancement. I am just peculiar. A gentle giant and a nobody.

I am trying to fit in. But even with assistance from Jude, Father Paul, and Claudia it took months to get free from the insanity of the Parker Home. How could someone like me, with a bizarre backstory, find a place in a clown-car-Keystone-Cops world? Maybe never. Even if I willingly signed up for the carnival, I would be forced to endlessly ride on the merry-go-round. I'm not optimistic, but I am trying, nonetheless.

Sadly, I know first-hand the worst features of organizational behavior. Matt's aversion to being seen, known, poked, and prodded, was well founded. Price's Law lives in the reality of organizations, and ones providing long-term care can be the cruelest. In such places, incompetence exponentially grows while competence grows linearly. Over time they become hell holes. Imagine what would have happened if a state-run 'healthcare facility' grabbed hold of a genius such as Matt. Imagine me there, too. That *Beast* had me, and I am so glad to have gotten away.

What is to be next?

I have never had a real home, but I am homesick for a place I have never been to or seen. When I was flying, I believe I was searching for that home.

It is said a man hurt enough to shed tears in public is the most secure, honest, and capable man in the world. I awake with tears that stain my face all day. Yet I am so sad and fear the unknown threats around me. I want to build a barrier and paint it haunt blue, like the Gullahs on the coast of South Carolina do to fend off evil spirits. Like them, I, too, want to create a spiritual boundary—to protect my sorrow-filled soul.

The highest honor that could be placed upon me is that Matthias Emanuel Mueller is my friend. I miss my friend, a wondrous-event person, with the mind of a genius, scorned for his physical form, yet imbued with the soul of an angel.

He told me, "God loved the Universe into existence. We can know him by becoming the best human being we can be."

He was right.

Was he a freak of nature? No. I believe he was a gift from the Creator, an example of transcendence being integral in consciousness. I remember Matt as being all the positives and none of the negatives in life—in everything.

Imagine the bluebird in Charles Bukowski's poem being freed—that was Matt—hiding in plain sight, a magical bluebird full of goodness and love.

Matt spoke of a path to be sought, known, and walked. I believe the path he spoke of is real and he left to complete his following it.

When I dream, I still hear him, "Truth does exist. Find it. Know it. Be the best you can be as you find your home."

Matt wanted me to become independent and to find my path.

I believe if I am successful, I may meet him, or his spirit, along the way.

* * *

THEY SAY CONSCIOUSNESS CAN ALTER space and time. Now is my time to do so—in finding my friend. But how do you find a someone who successfully hid from the world for his entire life?

My thought is the best clue will be found in Matt's own words. Often, he attributed his anonymity to hiding 'in plain sight'. I will focus on the word *plain*—The *Plain* People. I am certain, it is within the reclusive Amish community that Matt will be found.

Much of Amish country is an isolated island where one will find numerous outhouses, horse-drawn buggies, mules, no electricity, where kids are kids, and plenty of peace and quiet. The people are reserved and polite, but tight-lipped around outsiders. Shunning photographs, the wariest are organized within districts—each made up of only twenty-four families. The most conservative districts primarily conduct their dealings with the world by brokered long-time associations with Mennonites—another Plain People group. For an outsider, opening up the most reclusive districts is extremely difficult.

Surnames in Amish country are a quagmire. Imagine sifting for a lead through more than 300,000 individuals in closed groups where a limited number of names such as, Miller, Mueller, Lapp, King, Fisher, Beiler, and Stoltzfus are your options. The multiple spellings of names within the culture can be maddening. Stoltzfus alone has: Stoltzfus, Stoltzfuss, Stoltzfuz, Stoltz, Stolz, Stolze, Stoltze, Stolt, Stolte, Stoetzel, Stoltzel, Stolzel, Stolzer, Stollfus, and more as variations.

Rather than hunt only along that tack, I also studied geography. And again, it was Matt's words that indicated where to search. I poured over maps, adding his name, Mueller, into the mix. Mueller, Old Order, very conservative, and in close proximity to the Welsh Mountains is what I looked for.

Why there? Matt had an affinity, a love based on respect, for Native Americans. He often spoke with nostalgia for the Welsh Mountains, home of the Miqua, and the only location in Lancaster County with ties to the original inhabitants of Pennsylvania. Also, the Welsh Mountains has a long history as a hiding place.

In the past, lowlanders saw the Welsh Mountains as a lawless place. Where remnants of the Susquehannock, also known as Conestogas, sought refuge with the Miqua, after the 1763 massacre perpetrated by the infamous Paxton Boys. The Miqua were also joined by whites escaping the abuses of indentured service, and runaway slaves. In time, the three races mixed and became known simply as Miquas. Those who hid in the Welsh Mountains to avoid being killed, sent to reservations, or returned to slavery were, in their own opinion, not lawbreakers. In their minds, if any laws were broken, they were unjust ones that allowed abuse, slavery, and annihilation of native peoples.

After studying maps, I located an ideal spot Matt may have fled to. It was a patch of Amish land bordered on three sides by the Welsh Mountain Nature Preserve—a peninsula of sorts. I was certain Matt was there. Then I found a nearby district, residing very close, was a mix of Stoltzfus, Lapps, Beilers and Muellers.

I gave myself an enthusiastic high five—then quickly recalled outsiders are normally not welcomed to waltz across Amish farms. Gaining access to check out my hunch was not going to be easy unless I had an accomplice—like Father Paul Alexios.

I sat on pins and needles and waited for Father Paul to once again use his good standing with the plain folk. Easy Peasy—right? I needed him to smooth the path.

I got access, but nothing was there. No quaint little hideaway. No self-contained power source for a cabin that did not exist. There was nothing, absolutely nothing but farmland abutting the nature preserve. The Amish lad who accompanied me on my search was perplexed and amused by my quest into nowhere, to find someone who did not exist.

Matthias Mueller? Oh, yes. They knew him when he was the Down-Syndrome-looking, yet extremely able, visitor who hid within their district. But that was long ago, and they had not seen him in quite some time.

I failed. And that failure convinced me I had not been miraculously revived to become a detective. My purpose was elsewhere. If success was to come in finding Matt, it had to come from outside of my thoughts and abilities.

I thought I needed a definite, rock solid, more than vague, right-in-my-face, unmistakable, you can't miss it, *clue*. What I really needed in addition to a clue was directions.

Matt provided that clue and the directions by way of a simple plain postcard. And Jude completed its delivery.

"This is it." I exclaimed.

"But it's blank." Jude had no idea of what it was.

"No matter—it's from Matt."

"It has no message—there's nothing."

I pointed to the name, and then the postmark.

Jude was clueless.

"Who on earth is Zea Mays?" he asked.

"It's not *who*—it's *where.* And I am going there—
Now Now!"

The card, addressed to Zea Mays in care of
Sleeping Richard, bore Jude's home address.

The jokey description of me authenticated Matt as
the card's sender. It was postmarked by the regional
processing center in Dubuque, Iowa.

A clue and directions, as clear as could be.

* * *

LIKE MATT, I HAVE NEVER been far from Lancaster. Travel, other than dream-state flying, was an alien concept to me. However, Jude was an excellent teacher for the subject of *How to Travel*. After he thoroughly instructed me on the do's and dont's of mobility by bus, he graciously arranged all the details for me.

On the morning of departing on my quest (as my friends described 'my detective work'), Jude, Mya, and Father Paul joined together at the bus station to launch me on my way. The three of them fidgeted like parents sending their first-born off to kindergarten. They pitched in to supply me with a high-powered smart phone capable of searching the net, providing music, and playing audio books using earbuds.

Kisses, hugs, and a good many happy-sad tears flowed from the assembled's eyes. I boarded the bus with only a small backpack containing toiletries, extra socks, a change of underwear, a spare shirt, and my favorite book. I pressed the window tight with my face, waved goodbye, and was on my way.

My last thought in my hometown was one of guilt. I had not shared with my friends the return portion of my ticket would not be used. It nagged at my conscience I omitted that fact, but the guilt faded as the miles to reach Iowa waned.

On our way west, we—me and the bus, man and machine—were in tune, generally paralleling U.S. 30, the famous Lincoln Highway. It was dream-like—almost as good as flying. The beginning of a marvelous adventure.

I remember Matt telling me, "The *Velocity of Spirit* is how fast you go on your way home."

I was happy. I had a goal. I was traveling my path. I was like Kerouac on the road seeking Paradise with all the golden lands ahead and all kinds of unforeseen events lurking to surprise me.

* * *

FOR TWO DAYS I SAW nothing but corn, corn, and more corn. Did you know the corn belt spans more than twelve hundred miles across the United States? Thank goodness my trip was only through a portion of it. With pee breaks, meal stops, and so on, a complete trip across this wonder of modern farming could take four days or more by bus.

Books, newspapers, magazines, flyers, pamphlets—you name it and I read it. To rest my weary eyes, I hooked up an audio book. Even then, I heard his voice. I imagine the professional readers of audio books, paid good money for their voices, would be offended to learn about this. Maybe they already know, or suspect, the author is the star and they are the aftermarket afterthoughts of literature.

I miss Matt reading to me. Since my awakening, I have become a speed reader. When my eyes scan words, it is his voice I hear in my head. What voice do you hear?

I longed to hear Matt's voice again, so I began to read. The following story, picked up by a syndicator appeared in the paper I bought at one of our many stops, maybe it was in Minerva, Ohio.

The story was brief, in one of those tinted boxes on the page edge. Matt's voice confirmed what I learned from the postcard.

Wire feed, originally printed in the *Dubuque Register*—Sheriff's Department Ends Search—Carey Wells, spokesperson for the Dyersville Sheriff's Department, announced today, at a hastily called press briefing, the search for a missing visitor to the popular 'Field of Dreams' near Dyersville, has been stood down.

Ms. Wells briefly stated, "After a thorough search of the popular tourist destination's grounds, it has been concluded the unidentified visitor either departed the complex and its surroundings, or has been aided, by a person or persons unknown, to disappear.

"The department has not ruled out the possibility of the incident being a hoax, or an elaborate practical joke played upon the public. This conjecture is based upon several witnesses describing the alleged missing person as being a Down Syndrome individual who displayed obvious signs of intelligence much beyond that group's norms.

"In any event, we appreciate the staff at the facility for initially sounding the alarm."

* * *

I HAVE SHARED WITH YOU HOW Matt loved *Shoeless Joe*. From recalling the many readings of it, and the postcard, I knew exactly *where* I must go. Sadly, it was through his second favorite book, *I Heard The Owl Call My Name*, that I knew the *why* of his disappearance. Matt was dying. He had heard the owl call his name.

Before my departure, Claudia had warned me Matt's health was so fragile I may never see him again. I sensed his time indeed was short, and the final miles of my trip found my face again stained by tears. I was cried out by the time I arrived in Dubuque, Iowa. I was almost there—Dubuque to Dyersville is a thirty-mile cab drive.

The driver who picked me up at the bus station was a desert-dried prune with arms and legs, and a straight-from-central-casting geezer. Shorts, t-shirt, frayed ball cap and sunglasses made up his uniform, and as he drove, he constantly whistled, hummed, and mumbled to himself as the world passed by.

On the way, I looked at that world of endless corn and wondered how does a late-eightyish-year-old duffer end up driving a cab in Iowa.

I started a conversation.

"Like your job?"

"Yep—gets me out 'nd 'bout. Love meetin' folks 'nd seein' the world."

"That's good."

"Yep—it's my life 'nd I like it fine." His voice had a smile in it. Also comfort, optimism, and authentic cheer. "I'm okay with everythin' 'nd I'm hopin' it keeps go'n on. Got some good years 'n me."

He did not look it at first, but he was the perfect end-of-life poster boy for contentment. I was pleasantly surprised.

"Tell me your secret—how did you come to driving a cab and being so happy with it?"

"Long story—really wanna hear it?"

"Of course—tell me."

"I was born poor in South Indiana. Hated small towns, farms, you name it—wanted more. War come on th' heels of the Depression—th' Great one 'nd I joined up—at fifteen."

"Fifteen—that's young. Was it legal back then?"

"Nope. I'm what you call a veter'n of unnerage mil'try service. We even got a org'nazhun—VUMS."

"Did you see fighting? Combat?"

"Plenty—was in North Africa, Sic'ly, It'ly— landed at Anzio—that was a doozie of a mess.

Finished up in Germ'ny—after we fought 'em all way 'cross th' south of France."

"What happened to you after the war?"

"Bummed around th' whole world—just seen too much killin'. Had to get away—worked out th' bad. Come home in forty-nine. Got a job, a wife, kids 'nd lived best I could. She left me—took th' kids 'nd house—lost th' job, drank a ocean of alc'hol, sobered up after I met num'er two. From Jamaica. Black and beaut'ful as all get out. In them days, idyits 'round here thought we was crim'nals, probly crazy, too—being a mixed couple. But, she's as sweet as she is pleasin' on th' eye. She helped me 'n many ways through love. Built a good life doin' all sorts a jobs. Drivin' this buggy since they pushed me out for bein' too old at th' fact'ry pressin' parts. Old? I outlived most of them fools in charge." He spoke his smile and winked at me by way of the rear view. "Times change. I believe we can make th' world better a li'le bit at a time."

I smiled back. Then I realized I did not know his name. "Pardon me, I didn't ask—what's your name?"

"Edgar— Edgar Herr. Friends call me Eggs. How 'bout you?"

"Richard—I'm Richard."

"Good meetin' ya, Sonny."

"Same here, Eggs."

His brief story was so good I lost track of the reason I asked. "So, what's your secret?"

"I got rules—plus, I follow a simple plan. In life, never blame anyone—'nd no grudges. Remember, good people give you happiness 'nd love, th' bad ones give you experience at overcomin', 'nd th' best people give you th' ability to love. And love th' life you make—not th' one others might want for you."

"That is beautiful—absolutely beautiful."

"Maybe—th' real hard part is th' doin'. I tell folks—I ain't a good man—I'm just tryin' t' be one." Once more he spoke with his smile.

I responded by signing a 'thumbs up' for him to see through the rear view. I was awed by his optimism and simple goodness. I saw the chance of meeting him as a good omen. I was happy.

Soon I was back eyeballing the passing fields. All I could see were rows and rows of corn. Green, alive, and ubiquitous. At some point I muttered the name on the postcard, "Zea Mays."

"Your girlfriend? Name sounds foreign—she a foreigner?"

"No—it's a name, but not for a person."

"Sounds sorta foreign-like. You know—exotic."

A small chuckle slid out of me, "It's a name for corn."

* * *

A LITTLE PAST NOON, EGGS AND I arrived at my destination.

"Here we are, Sonny. Want me to wait? Only be an extra twenty."

I told him, "Eggs, there's no need to wait."

"No trouble for me—"

"I won't need a ride back, Eggs." I didn't mean to cut him off, but I admit I was more than a little excited.

"Okay. You meetin' someone?"

"You could say so. At least, I hope to."

I wish there was a photo of me. My smile had to be 'glow-in-the-dark' bright. It's a good thing he was wearing shades. The radiance would have blinded him. I handed him the fare, accompanied by a healthy tip.

"Whoa—Sonny. I don't charge for life coachin'. All I say is just me talkin' and if I thought I would be taken serious, I might not talk at all."

I motioned for him to keep all the money. He said, "Okay, but here's 'nother freebie. In life things happen for no reason at all—unless you give 'em a reason." He punctuated his advice with a wink.

I had to ask. "Eggs—do you know your shirt is inside-out?"

"Yeah—I wear it like this when I want the day to go different—when I need a miracle to happen. Which is pretty much every day. I believe in miracles—big ones, little ones, and the kind that stretch on forever."

We shook hands, and he said, "Sonny—I mean Richard—hope you find ev'rthin' you're lookin' for. I hope you find a miracle."

Then he drove away. At the exit, he leaned halfway out his window and shot me a victory sign.

The experience of meeting Eggs taught me it was possible to make a friend almost instantly. Eggs, the Ancient Cabbie, Guru-in-Shorts and an inside-out T-shirt, and my new best friend was one of the good people.

Sadly, I found myself alone. Yet I suspected my condition would soon change.

* * *

THE FIELD LOOKS MUCH AS it did in the movie. Sure, they added a gift shop, but it is small, and it suitably matches the outbuildings and barn. A white picket fence skirts the house. *To herd tourists? Maybe. But what did they expect? If you build it, they will come.*

The mid-August sun is blazing. No clouds mar the sky. No shadows shade the corn. Nothing defining the outfield, or the beyond. I breathe it all in. Yet not for long. The end of my journey is but a few yards away. My goal awaits me.

I tingle.

I walk across center field, pausing at its out-most edge. An ever-so-slight breeze creeps past me to enter the rows and tease the corn.

Leaning toward the corn, I whisper, "Matt?"

A reply comes.

Is it just the rustling of corn? Soft laughter? A familiar voice? Or, is it merely sounds in my head? I strain to listen.

I hear a voice. I have hope. But doubt quickly follows—assaults my castle wall of faith.

Matt told me many times, "If you can move mountains, but have no faith, you have nothing at all."

I close my eyes—hearing his voice speak to me from the ether that is the past.

Now, I hear Matt say, "Every moment you live has but two possible next moments. One is final, the other has infinite possibilities."

The sound is back in contrast. Unidentifiable. Familiar. Mixed. Pure. Classic. Experimental. *Music?*

No—the sighs of being. Louder. Clearer—more defined. Real. Right. Just. True. Truer than any Truth experienced or imagined. Truer than the Truth. Possible?

Is this his *voice—from the special place that is no place at all?*

My eyes remain closed. Yet I can still see—with my heart. Before me are all the dreams, hopes, and yearnings of every being that was, is, or ever shall be. It is the oneness in which I will participate.

A single word emerges from the rows of corn.

"Come."

One word. That is enough.

The fabric of the Universe splits open. Zero Point Energy escapes—dances throughout my body. My essence—my being, my me-ness—sees, feels, absorbs, and experiences the infinite goodness of that which is beyond life, love, space, time, and my very existence.

I stare at a wall of green.

Many times, when Matt read to me, I saw it in my imagination. Now, with it before me, I am consumed with curiosity to know something old in a new way. The space between the nearest two rows forms a narrow gateway to my future.

Doubt has no place within me.

I enter the corn.

* * *

HELLO AGAIN!

YOU'RE BACK. THAT TRULY MAKES me happy, because I was beginning to wonder if you were real or just in my imagination.

Which leads me to ask—If you are real, how and why are you here? And, are you curious about what happened in the cornfield?

* * *

A FEW FEET INSIDE THE FIELD, my steps ended. I was in a silent space. There was no music. No rustling corn. No wind. No voices. No sound at all. Just me. One might call it an eerie sort of sacred place. It felt that way.

Did I bathe in spiritual bliss? No.

I was simply aware of that moment…and every moment preceding…and beyond. I have no idea how long it was just me and the corn. The stillness one finds at the end of expectation has an eternal quality. I found myself on the cusp of the real and imagined—a place where the material universe meets the spiritual realm.

Did I experience eternity within a millionth of a microsecond? Beats me. I do not know if time even exists in such a place. Maybe timeless is better description. At some point I became aware of my thoughts and took stock of the situation.

Remarkably, not finding Matt did not disturb me. I was alone in a cornfield, brought there by way of a movie set turned tourist attraction—a commercial venture built to exploit a sentimental popular myth. Just the sort of playful nudge Matt's ironic sense of humor would produce.

It had everything he loved—baseball, dreams, and me wishing for the magical to be real. So, where was Matt? Whose hand was in this?

My mind latched upon an ancient verse of scripture. "Enoch walked with God; then he was no more, because God took him."

Serious stuff—or could it just be an experiential Matt Fact—a joke—or a lesson?

Matt had lured me out of Lancaster, prompted me on a quest. And I have succeeded in finding and then transcending my goal. Matt had been a diminutive intellectual Merman, gliding through a sea of thoughts, snatching one in his mouth, consuming it, digesting its value, transforming it to a shell, spitting it upon the sand for me to place at my ear. Oh, the roars I hear.

I have come to know that our universe is merely a shadow of a greater reality, and that my life is a reflection of its existence—one found through experience.

Filled with joy, I shout into a crimson tinted sky, "*Thank You*, Matt. I understand. I love you—and I know we'll meet again."

But it is my time now.

I pause to collect myself, and ponder becoming Future Me.

What will I do?

I must be more than what I already am—Matt's morphic resonance. I must wax after his waning. A student must strive to exceed the master.

Like Matt, I will not stand in the circumstances in which I was born. I will inch ever upward. My new quest will be to look forward, never back—always moving, absorbing life, transcending Matt's influence, experiencing the wonder of *my* being. Living each day with joyful purpose. Knowing that every moment is a pivotal one. Seeking not to only build a life, but to savor it fully. Guarding my essence with diligence. Believing in the holy contour of existence—demonstrating, as did Novalis, that the longest way 'round is the shortest way home—to the Creator's House.

For some few—no explanation is needed. For those who cannot, or refuse to understand, no amount of explanation will suffice. But nonetheless I will try to explain.

Experience teaches. One must consume life with Zorba's passion. Seek the wonders of being. Understand heaven is a gift, not a reward. Walk into the corn. Read a book. Explore Neverland. Treasure those who love you. Listen to those with whom you disagree.

Understand you'll never outperform your belief system. Do not degrade faith by practicing religion. Sing. Cry. Fight. Laugh. Love. Forget your mantra. Live, recognizing that *being* is an adventure that transcends understanding your very existence. Live beyond consensus reality. Ponder eternity. Pray. Seek God.

The list, as long as you imagine it to be, will guide you along the razor's edge of consciousness. Catch up with the truth that is waiting for you by conducting each moment as a ceremony of life. But beware, we are so easily distracted.

The truth is not told, it is learned as you live a quality-filled life that keeps on happening because you are interested in it. Be bold and mighty forces will come to your aide.

Proceed—I'll know how you fare. Remember, I am in your mind.

Epilogue

BROADCAST TRANSCRIPT OF **KFXB-TV DUBUQUE, Iowa:**

"Good evening—I'm Jean Corpus, and here is the news.

"Earlier today, residents west of Dubuque were treated to a unique event in the summer sky. A reverse rainbow—a circumzenithal arc, a CZA—was observed shortly after noon in the sky west of the city.

"A CZA is like a common rainbow except that it appears opposite the sun and is upside-down. It's vibrantly colored, with separated hues, purer than those of a typical rainbow—and very few people have ever observed one of these spectacular events. For more, let's go to Ben Wicker on the scene."

"Ben, what have people seen?" [Cut to Ben.]

"Hi, Jean. I'm on site near Dyersville, where residents and visitors have experienced what many are calling miraculous. We reached out to the U.S. Weather Bureau where meteorologists have simply, but accurately, stated that, 'This type phenomenon is beautiful and extremely rare.' In search for more colorful comments (a chuckle), we have sought out folks who witnessed the actual display for their reactions."

[Cut to clip of Edgar Herr, local taxi driver.]

[Name and occupation seen below the image.]

"It was sumpin' to see awe-right. An upside-down rainbow, colors deeper 'nd richer than reg'lar. Touched the ground somewhere out there in the corn."

[Back to Ben.]

"Jean, we even have a picture of this wonder. Loraine Peters, a visiting tourist headed to the popular *Field of Dreams* captured this spectacular event."

[Cut to image, with a voice over by Loraine, pictured in lower box.]

"Yeah, it was beautiful. We were driving into the site, and I just looked up. My husband stopped the car, and I used my phone to snap a shot. It was amazing."

[Cut back to Ben.]

"Yes, amazing, Jean. Some people call it what it is—a miracle."

* * *

ABOUT THE AUTHOR

DEL STAECKER IS AN AMERICAN writer of novels, novellas, short stories, and non-fiction in a number of genres, including suspense, crime, philosophical fiction, satire, and memoir.

He is a Life Fellow of the Royal Society of Arts (London) and Knight of Honor, Order of St. John (Malta). He was educated at The Citadel, Wheaton College, and The University of Puget Sound.

OTHER WORKS BY THIS AUTHOR

NON-FICTION

*The Lady Gangster: A Sailor's Memoir
(2009) ISBN 978-1934980224*

*Sailor Man: The Troubled Life and Times of J.P.
Nunnally, USN (2015) ISBN 978-1555718169*

FICTION

The Muted Mermaid (2008) ISBN 978-0979949463

Shaved Ice (2008) ISBN 978-1934980125

Chocolate Soup (2010) ISBN 978-1934980576

Tales of Tomasewski (2012) ISBN 978-1619373693

More Tomasewski (2014) ISBN 978-1619373709

One Good Man (2016) ISBN 978-1945772177

*Job 2.0: God and Lucifer Battle Again for a
Single Soul (2019) ISBN 978-0310107583*

CPSIA information can be obtained
at www.ICGtesting.com
Printed in the USA
BVHW060208050222
627508BV00006B/12